In *Confessions to a Stranger*, Danielle Grandinetti weaves a tale that is at once mysterious, suspenseful, romantic, and inspiring ... Filled with truths that made me ponder my own life, this novel is a lovely start to what is sure to be a wonderful series!

—Heidi Chiavaroli,
Carol Award-Winning Author of *The Orchard House*

Danielle Grandinetti has crafted a wonderful tale of suspense and romance that will keep you on the edge of your seat. With well-drawn characters authentic to the era, a gripping plot, and a strong message of hope, *Confessions to a Stranger* is a read I recommend!

—Misty M. Beller,
USA Today bestselling author of the Sisters of the Rockies

A Strike to the Heart is a compelling story. From the very first page, I was immersed into the thrilling action and remained gripped with intrigue until the satisfying ending.

The romance escalated right along with the winding plot, creating a layered mystery that is sure to delight readers.

—Rachel Scott McDaniel,
Award-winning author of *The Mobster's Daughter*

Riveting from the first scene, *As Silent as the Night* offers a unique, edge-of-your-seat Christmas read ... A beautiful, gripping, and romantically suspenseful Christmas story you wouldn't be able to put down if you tried.

—Chautona Havig,
Author of *The Stars of New Cheltenham*

The Neighbor and the Gifts is a poignant tale that transforms a familiar carol into a stirring journey of faith, love, and danger ... For readers who love historical romance, mystery, and want a deeper meaning in their holiday stories—this one's for you.

—Natalie Walters,
bestselling and award-winning author of *Living Lies* and the *SNAP Agency* series

The RECLUSE'S VINDICATION

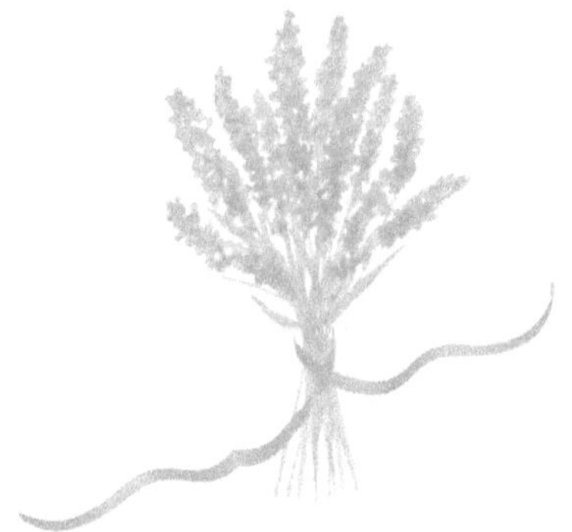

Danielle Grandinetti

The Recluse's Vindication

Rumors, Monsters, and Second Chances at Our House on Heather Wynd

Danielle Grandinetti

Hearth Spot Press

To my international readers and friends.

Especially Anna Jensen and Caroline Johnston who have coordinated this multi-author, multi-genre series. You both have become sweet friends through the Our House projects. I'm blessed to know you and hope we can meet one day, whether on my continent or one of yours.

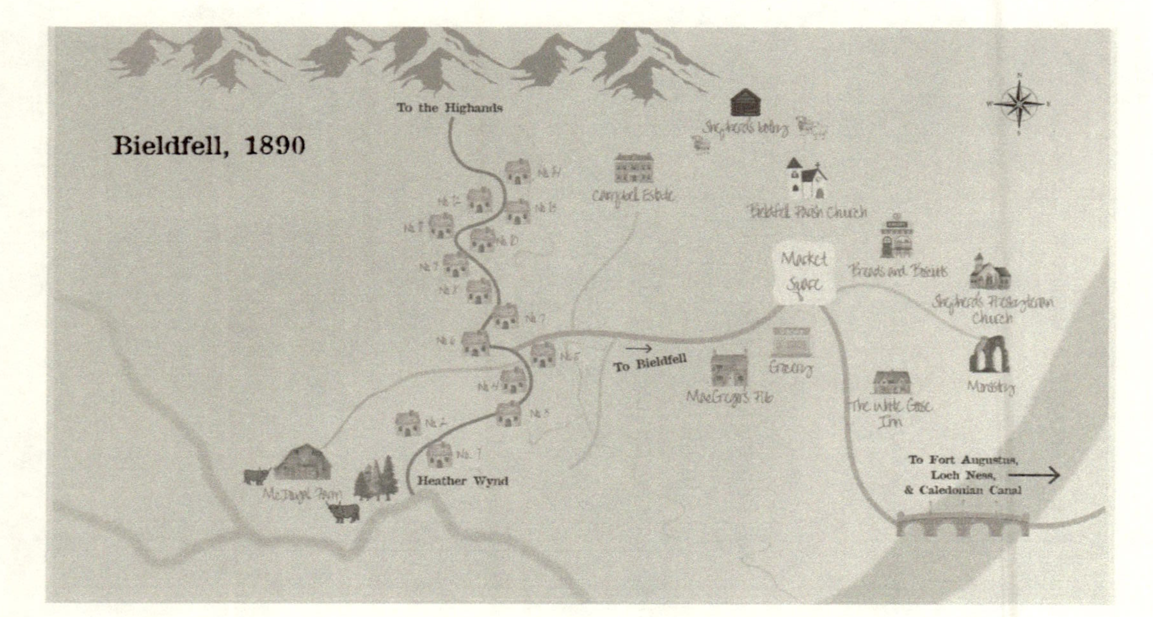

Bieldfell, 1890
To the Highands
Shepherd's bothy
Campbell Estate
Bieldfell Parish Church
Market Square
Breads and Biscuits
Shepherd's Presbyterian Church
Monastery
MacGregor's Pub
Grocery
The White Goose Inn
To Bieldfell
Heather Wynd
McDougal Farm
To Fort Augustus, Loch Ness, & Caledonian Canal

But Jesus said, Suffer little children, and
forbid them not, to come unto me: for of
such is the kingdom of heaven.
Matthew 19:14, KJV

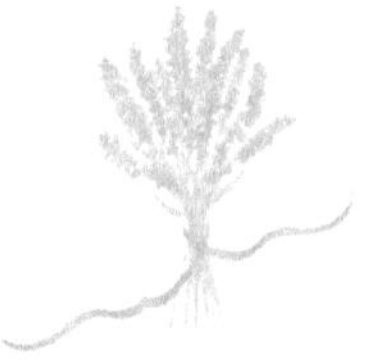

Chapter One

Scottish Highlands near Fort Augustus

Benjamin Ford stood atop a hill cloaked in a mist that hid him from God Himself and his fellow man. Head bowed under the weight of his sins, they pressed on his broad shoulders. But he would carry them if it meant an innocent would live.

The cool dampness swirled around him. The lapping of Loch Ness below created an otherworldly sense. There was life beyond the veil. Today, he didn't want to acknowledge it. Perhaps because yesterday, he'd taken a thirty-fourth life. The exact number of years he'd lived on this earth.

Or maybe because today heralded the sixteenth anniversary of the first time he killed a man.

What absolution could there be for a man with so much bloodshed on his hands? He opened them now, his sleeves rolled to his elbows, revealing the tattoos gained from his time in the US Navy. Droplets formed on weather-worn skin, the mist heavy with water. It couldn't wash away the darkness that threatened to crush his soul.

"Herr Ford?" a tiny voice preceded the equally tiny child.

"Yes, Amalie?" Benjamin switched to German before kneeling before the brave little orphan girl he'd smuggled out of Germany last night. Her blond hair hung limp about her pale face. "Are you ready to see Miss Blair? She'll have tea and biscuits."

"Will I like my new home?" Her blue eyes shimmered. The poor girl had lost so much in a few short hours, stolen by men who thought her Jewish blood made her less than they. "I don't want to leave you."

"Oh, wee one." His voice roughened as she slipped into his embrace. He had promised her father, his friend, that he would do all in his power to protect the man's only child. But she deserved more than the damaged soul of the likes of him.

Benjamin clenched his jaw against the anger that welled within him. Abe Klein and his wife were good people. Amalie's father, a university professor, helped bring peace to his country after the Great War, which is how Ben first met the man. Then, earlier this year, Chancellor Hitler was elected and turned the government inside out, and Abe turned to providing intelligence to the Brits, using Ben as a go-between.

Amalie whimpered, and Ben pressed her head against his chest. When word came that Jewish children would no longer be allowed to attend school, Abe planned to send his wife and daughter to Scotland with Ben while staying to fight against the coming evil. Only, Ben was too late for his friend and his wife. He'd had to kill to save Amalie, then whisk her and the information her father died to protect out of Germany.

For this innocent child, he hadn't hesitated to do what had to be done. He couldn't hesitate now. He tugged Amalie so he could see her tear-stained face. "Miss Agnes loves children, you know."

"Will I stay with her?" The little girl swiped at her cheeks.

That wasn't the plan, but Ben reconsidered as he used his massive thumbs to catch two errant tears that sped down her cheeks. "Shall we ask her?"

Agnes Blair was a wizened, elderly lady with contacts within US and British intelligence most would never believe, and the reason he'd lived on the edge of Loch Ness these past ten years. Technically, he worked for the US military. Still, should he be captured smuggling innocents and information out of countries like Germany, Italy, and Russia, he'd be disowned and left to face likely execution. Not that he cared. He was expendable.

"I wish I could stay with you." She rested her tiny hand on his, and his heart cracked. What had he done to deserve the trust of this child?

He shouldered the ruck he'd retrieved from his shepherd's hut on the hill, and they walked together down toward Bieldfell, a small hamlet outside Fort Augustus, leaving the mist behind.

Agnes lived in number seven, right in the middle of Heather Wynd. Her small cottage was set back from the road and framed by a bright burst of pink cherry blossoms.

She opened her door as soon as they stepped onto her cobblestone path.

"Welcome!" Her Scottish accent rounded her words.

Amalie tightened her hold on Ben's hand. He squeezed her little fingers as they entered Agnes's home. The cobblestone floor had been swept clean. The high rafters held up the thatch roof and skeins of dyed yarn. Only one window left the room dark, with a thick smell of peat. Walking inside always felt like being transported to days gone by.

He waited until Agnes closed the door. "I've brought a new friend."

"Indeed." Agnes leaned on her cane, a smile deepening the wrinkles that lined her round face. Her gray hair was pinned at the back of her head, and her spectacles highlighted soft green eyes. "What is your name, child?"

Amalie looked up at Ben. He knelt and wrapped his arm over her shoulder. "Amalie Klein, this is Miss Agnes Blair. Miss Agnes, Amalie only knows German."

"Ah." Agnes tapped her cheek with a bent finger. He didn't know how she continued to spin wool with the pain in her hands, but he would bring her wool until she could no longer support herself, and then he'd take on her care.

"Perhaps Amalie will teach me German, and I will teach her English?"

Ben translated while giving Agnes a quizzical look. Agnes spoke fluent German, but that wasn't the point. Amalie staying here wasn't the plan, and not until Amalie had suggested it had he even considered leaving Amalie here instead of delivering her to a family who could keep her safe.

"Ja." Amalie nodded, then fired rapid German at him.

Ben stood. "She wants to stay with me, but that is not feasible. I leave at a moment's notice, and my hut is no place for a little girl."

"She'll stay here, of course." Agnes had this way about her: there would be no argument when she issued a declaration.

"No offense, Agnes, but can you manage a seven-year-old who doesn't share your language?"

"We won't know until we try, right?" Agnes held out her aged hand to Amalie, who left Ben's side to let Agnes escort her to the wooden table where a plate of cookies sat.

Ben stayed back, watching the pair. Through hand movements and animated expressions, they struck up a conversation over shared cookies and tea. Ben inched toward the door. This was right. Good, even. Then why did it pang him to leave? He needed to catch the train down to London to deliver his report, a fact Agnes knew well.

Yet, watching this scene reminded him of what—whom—he'd left behind in Montana sixteen years ago. He could almost picture her joining Agnes and Amalie at the table here. She would welcome this child without question. Eleanor Finch had been his dearest friend until he'd killed the banker's son. Then he'd left so she wouldn't be tainted by being acquainted with a man people called a murderer.

Agnes met his gaze across the room, no doubt seeing more than he wished. She also wouldn't let him leave without a goodbye.

As he kissed the top of Amalie's head, his resolve strengthened. Evil was building on the Continent. The grandson of a beast, the son of a monster, a man who had already killed with his bare hands. He would accept the mantle God laid on him and trade his soul so the innocent could live.

Chapter Two

Sunday, April 30, 1933

Blue Spruce, Montana

Eleanor kept to the edges of the church building to avoid getting trapped within the knots of people as they spilled into the fresh spring air. She hated the pitying looks, the suspicion, even the disgust, but not enough to avoid the house of God. Only a few more steps and she could escape to the boarding house.

A hand grabbed her elbow. She spun to slap the offender, only for the strike to be blocked by a feminine glove. Breath rushed out of Eleanor. "Mrs. Ward, you startled me."

"I'm sorry for that." Cora Ward wrapped Eleanor's hand around her arm, her black ringlets bouncing about her tanned face as she led them toward the exit. "I know how much you dislike being singled out, but I need you to accompany Silas and me back to Crooked Tooth."

Fragile hope squeezed her chest. "You found something."

Cora pressed her lips together, blue eyes dancing.

"You found *him*."

Cora propelled them out the church door.

Cora's husband, Silas, had returned to Blue Spruce two years ago with wife in tow, taking up his old position as a ranch hand for Benjamin's grandfather. Unable to stay on the ranch with Silas, Cora defied the town's gossips by becoming Eleanor's friend. Eleanor had poured out more of her story to Cora than she had to anyone else. Not even Ben or her mama—God rest her soul—knew *everything*.

But Eleanor owed Cora even more. When Silas became foreman, she moved to Crooked Tooth Ranch, leaving Eleanor at the mercy of the busybodies. Not for long, however. When the wife of Silas's late brother arrived in

Blue Spruce with her family and new mother-in-law, Cora introduced them. So when the older Mrs. Cox started up a boardinghouse, Eleanor became the cook with room and board as part of her wages, protecting her from wandering without a home.

Now, Cora had gone the extra mile. No, an extra thousand miles. And somehow found Ben. Eleanor yearned to ask the questions burning inside, but Cora gave her no time. Silas swung their toddling boy up to the wagon seat before swiftly lifting Cora in time to catch the little one before his curiosity had him reaching for the horsey's tail. Silas smiled at Eleanor as he helped her up to the bench beside his wife. For a serious, intense man, he was kind and utterly adored his wife and child.

Eleanor hugged her waist. Ben had once looked at her with a similar expression as Silas did Cora. Or was that her imagination? Memory was fuzzy sixteen years later. He remained her hero, though. He'd saved her life, even though it meant taking that of the man attacking her. Not that George Brown, or the rest of the gossips, believed her story.

Cora kept up a stream of chatter about a recent visit with a Blackfoot woman whose story she was chronicling. Eleanor supposed listening would be polite, but she couldn't concentrate when she was minutes away from learning what had become of Ben. The boy—no, man—had disappeared without a trace. His grandfather, a wealthy rancher, had hired detectives to find him. But the Great War had stymied them, and there had been no trace.

How had Cora found him?

Silas halted the wagon in the yard of Crooked Tooth Ranch. Eleanor frequently visited to see Cora but hadn't set foot in the main house for years. Ben had grown up here, and they had traipsed together over the land from here to the mountains. Silas helped her and Cora down from the wagon before lifting his son to his shoulders and handing the wagon team to a waiting ranchhand. On the porch steps, Ben's grandparents waited for them, arm-in-arm.

Eleanor hesitated. Mrs. Orson always spoke kindly to her, but Mr. Orson was a bear of a man, even larger than Silas. The gossips all called him a beast, not that there was any truth to their barbs. Still, he intimidated her. And while neither showed any sign of hostility toward her, Eleanor had always wondered if they might harbor even a slight resentment toward her for being the reason their grandson was accused of murder and disappeared.

"Come, El." Cora dragged her toward the porch steps. "The Orsons know as much as you because I only wish to explain this once. It's a convoluted tale."

But Eleanor's feet slowed as she came face-to-face with Ben's grandparents. Mrs. Orson, a well-regarded horse handler, appeared gaunt and pale. Mr. Orson's jaw shifted with the intensity of his eyes. Words froze in Eleanor's throat.

"Are you sure it's him?" Mr. Orson stared down Cora.

"She's sure, boss." Silas, with his son on his shoulders, ducked to keep from bumping his son's head on the porch roof. "Her source, as winding as it may sound, is impeccable."

"Men." Cora rolled her eyes. "Can't take me at my word, but have to bicker about it. Come, ladies, and I'll share what I found."

"She has a point, my love." Mrs. Orson gave her husband the side-eye, then hooked her arm around Eleanor's. "I wouldn't want to hear this without you, dear. You need this as much as we do."

Eleanor blinked back the tears. "What if he's not the same Ben that we knew?" That had always been her deepest fear, and embarrassment washed over her as it slipped between her lips.

"One step at a time, child." Mrs. Orson hugged Eleanor's arm as if the words were as much for her as herself.

Once they'd gathered in the simple parlor, Cora began her tale. Mrs. Orson kept hold of Eleanor as they sat together on the sofa. Mr. Orson paced like a lion as she spoke. And Silas jostled and entertained their son so Cora could give her speech uninterrupted.

"You know I used to be an archaeologist." Cora folded her hands in her lap. "I worked on a dig in Italy, which is where I met a trio of sweet young women. One tragically lost her life in the earthquake that brought me back to the States, another escaped to England to avoid persecution at the hands of Mussolini's Blackshirts, and the third joined her brother, Dr. Matrone, in Silas's old hometown."

"Why do we need to know all that?" Mr. Orson grunted.

"Hush, love." Mrs. Orson swatted at him.

Eleanor bit her lip, agreeing with Ben's grandfather that she wished Cora would hurry up. Though she knew of Dr.

Matrone, seeing that the man often offered Cora medical advice when one of her spells landed her in bed.

"For the past year, I've sent letters to all my contacts within the archaeological community. It's small, but no one had any rumor of a Benjamin Ford." Cora inclined her head toward Mr. Orson. "Until I mentioned my dilemma to my friend Dr. Matrone. He offered to ask around on my behalf as well. Wouldn't you know, I had the connection all along?"

"The trio of girls?" Mrs. Orson leaned forward.

Cora nodded, excitement brightening her countenance. "Bella and Margherita still write letters, and Margherita has a contact who knows Ben."

"Are they sure it's our Ben?" Mr. Orson came to stand at his wife's side. "What if this is a false lead?"

Cora met each of their gazes. "Because the contact is looking for you three."

Eleanor's heart thumped. The contact was looking, not Ben. Ben didn't want to be found.

"Then we must go at once." Mrs. Orson covered her face. "Our Benjy. Our innocent Benjy."

Mr. Orson knelt beside his wife. "Where is he?"

"Scotland."

"So far?" Mrs. Orson turned into her husband's shoulder.

"We will find a way, love."

Eleanor stared at her lap. The Orsons couldn't leave their ranch, not on such a journey. What if this wasn't Ben? They'd be heartbroken. Not to mention, at their age, such travel could cost them dearly. But Eleanor? She had nothing to lose. No, she owed the family this for all they sacrificed because of her.

"I'll go." The words jumped out with more conviction than she expected.

"What?" Mrs. Orson turned teary eyes upon her.

"Not alone, you won't," Mr. Orson commanded.

"Sir, if I may?" Silas plopped his son in Cora's lap. "When Cora told me the news, we anticipated this dilemma. We suggest Hiram go as Eleanor's chaperone. He can pose as her grandfather."

Eleanor startled. "You expected me to offer to go?"

"Of course, El." Cora tickled her son's neck. "Never a doubt in my mind."

"Hiram is a wise choice." Mr. Orson rose. "And Ben will trust him."

Hiram, who had no last name, was the oldest ranch hand left on the property. He still worked for the Orsons, but more in an honorary capacity these days. At one time, however, young Ben had been the man's shadow, and he a better father than Ben's actual one.

Cora exchanged a glance with Silas, a red hue darkening her complexion. "We, uh, we already made arrangements. El, you and Hiram need to catch the first train out tomorrow to New York, where you'll catch a steamer to London. From there, you'll travel to Fort Augustus in Scotland. The tickets have already been bought and paid for. All you need to do is pack."

A bubble of excitement rose within Eleanor. It dodged fear, and worry, and hope, and anticipation to emerge as a grin. She was going to Scotland to bring Benjamin Ford home to his family. She could only hope he would welcome seeing her again.

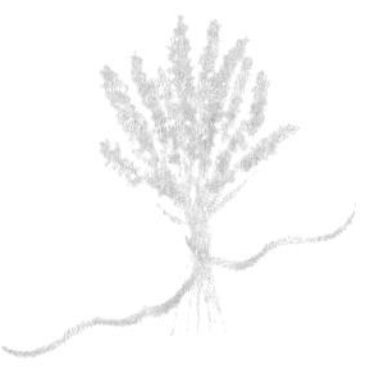

Chapter Three

"Did you hear there was another sighting?" An older lady leaned over the shop counter in Bieldfell's grocers, her attempt at a whisper falling far short. "Mrs. Mackay, over at the Drumnadrochit Hotel, saw that whale-like beast in the loch again."

Ben clenched the bag of salt in his hand to keep from reacting. Ever since Mrs. Mackay saw the whatever-it-was in Loch Ness a month ago, it was all anyone could talk about.

Mrs. Allan, the shopkeeper's wife, gasped as the customer no doubt expected. "Do you think going out on the Loch is safe with a fiend swimming about?"

Ben pinned his mouth shut when he wanted to ask why they immediately thought the whale-fish was a *fiend*. Were they scared of it because of its size? Because it was unknown? Why not exercise curiosity? Knowing a few fishermen hereabouts, their so-called curiosity would be to bring the whale-fish in, dead or alive, so they could dissect it. He rubbed his neck. When had he gotten so cynical? No need to answer that. War and espionage would do that to a man.

"I don't know, but I'm sure it's dangerous." The customer set down her coins to pay for her groceries. "Something like that could capsize a boat."

Ben set his bag of salt on the counter, debating whether he should point out that the speculation was pointless. The whale-fish hadn't attacked anyone, hadn't done anything but appeared a time or two. For all they knew, it could be a myth.

"It's a monster for sure." Mrs. Allan returned the change to the lady while keeping her eye on Ben. "Have a good day, Mrs. Wallace."

Mrs. Wallace hung her shopping bag from her arm but sidled slowly toward the door. "Should I stay?" she whispered loudly.

Embarrassment washed over him. He should be used to this reaction by now, and knew he did nothing to dissuade it. Perhaps that's why he felt so defensive of the Loch Ness whale-fish?

He cleared his throat. "Just this today, Mrs. Allan. Miss Blair asked me to bring it by for her." Now, why had he felt the need to add that last bit?

The women watched him closely as he paid for the salt. He used slow motions to avoid startling them, then escaped out the door like a little boy scolded for getting sticky hands on the fine china. He should have gotten candy for Amalie. Did he dare go back inside?

A big man like him, scared of what those ladies would say about him? He spun on his heel and reentered the shop. Both Mrs. Allan and Mrs. Wallace yipped at his entrance. He refused to cower. He'd lived outside Bieldfell for years, and they should be used to him by now. Or had the new sea creature rattled everyone this much?

"I forgot to get a package of lemon drops." He snagged the package.

Mrs. Allan rang it up. "For that dear sweet girl? She makes Miss Blair very happy."

He hadn't worked for government intelligence as long as he had without learning to pick up subtext. Mrs. Allan was fishing for information with a subtle barb lacing her words.

"Thank you, ma'am." Benjamin thickened the Montana drawl of his youth and tipped his imaginary cowboy hat. The women stared after him as he made his exit. With his back to them, he allowed a grin.

The good humor lasted all the way to number seven. He even had the rare opportunity to smile at a little boy as he played with a nanny in the garden. Two or three years old, he'd guess, the tike had the cheekiest grin. His parents were new to Heather Wynd, having bought the monstrosity of a house next door to Agnes. They kept to themselves, though he'd heard plenty from the gossips. Something about having it all, and still not being happy, or whispers of pity for the wife. Agnes, however, was tight-lipped about the little family and Ben let her have her secrets.

He rapped on Agnes's door before opening it with a greeting. A squeal sounded from inside, similar yet different from the ladies at the grocery. Before he could fully brace himself, a flurry of blonde braids and scrawny limbs crashed into him. He stumbled back a step, then dropped the salt and lemon drops to lift Amalie into the air.

"How's my kleine mädchen?" He spun her once before returning her to her feet and waving at Agnes, who watched them from the stove.

"I am good." Amalie beamed.

Ben grinned and dropped to one knee. "English, Amalie? You are learning so quickly."

She nodded, then switched to rapid German. "Miss Agnes teaches me, and I teach her German. We have fun. She cooks a lot, too. Different food, but it's still yummy. I missed you."

He wrapped an arm around her shoulders, struck again at the difference between his brawny, tattooed limb and her ... tininess. She hadn't used to be this thin. "Are you eating well?"

She rested her head on his shoulder. "My belly fills fast. Miss Agnes is making me ... *biscuits*." She sounded out the word in English.

"*Cookies*?" Ben winked. "That's what I call them because when I was your age, I lived in another country, too."

"You did?" Amalie hesitated, glancing down at her shoes. "Did you have to leave?"

Ben's heart panged. "Not like you, sweet one."

"Do you miss your mom and dad?"

He pulled her into a hug. Yeah, he missed his mom, but there was no way he could be anything but grateful his father was dead. "Your mom and dad were wonderful people, Amalie. They stood up to the bad men who thought hurting people was okay. That is why we need people like your mom and dad." People who could have protected his mom from people like his dad.

"But they were hurt, too." Amalie's voice was small.

"Yes." How could he explain this when he couldn't fully understand it? He'd stood up to Georgie Brown, protecting Eleanor like he wished someone could have done for his mother. However, instead of being lauded as a hero, he'd been accused of murder and forced to flee the country before Mr. Brown hunted him down. "I suppose the best explanation is that bad men are bullies, and bullies don't like it when people don't listen to them."

Amalie nodded, silent for a full minute. Ben held her, determined to stay there until she felt comforted enough, though his knee throbbed from leaning on the hard floor. Miss Agnes watched them with teary eyes. She knew why he'd joined the Navy, why he offered himself to intelligence work, why he hid himself in a small shepherd's hut overlooking Loch Ness.

"Mr. Ben?" Amalie leaned over his arm. "Are those lemon drops?"

Ben laughed at the change of topics. "Yes, they are, and I got them just for you."

She squealed, her sorrow forgotten as she snatched up the bag and snuggled onto the chair beside the window to indulge. He pushed to his feet, not quite as easily able to shed the memories of home. If Georgie's father was dead, perhaps he could ... visit?

"You will make a wonderful father someday, Ben." Miss Agnes opened the oven to remove a pan. "And these are biscuits, not cookies. Why do you Americans use that word?"

"To get on your nerves, of course." He set the salt on the counter, then leaned against the table, crossing his arms, grateful she'd let that first comment go.

Being a father would never be his lot. First of all, it required a wife and the only woman he ever loved—still loved, if he were honest—he'd left behind in Montana. After all these years, surely she was married and had a passel of kids running about. No, he could never return to Blue Spruce, even if the stain of murder didn't rest over his head. It would hurt too much to see how she had moved on when, on his loneliest nights, he dreamed of what could have been.

Secondly, his work would bring too much danger to a family. With the world resting on the edge of a knife, caught between economic disaster in America and rising trouble in Italy and now Germany, it was better to remain a bachelor. Expendable. Able to protect others without having to weigh the cost to himself or someone he loved.

Agnes eyed him as she shifted the kettle to the front burner.

"Any news for me?" Ben shifted their conversation to work before Agnes could express her opinion. He knew what she thought of him avoiding home.

"Mhmm." Agnes plated the cookies. "I received a coded letter from Reverend Charles down in Eden Cove. Luke Ferryman has agreed to transport refugees up the

River Deben, so we now have a coastal entry for the underground."

"Good. Calais to Dover is too closely watched." He knew Agnes had some sort of connection to the small town just northeast of the usual crossing between England and France. Eden Cove was located on the North Sea across from The Netherlands. "So if I can get them across the channel, can Ferryman and the reverend take over from there?"

"And he'll have papers from the Home Office ready for the refugees." Agnes handed him a cookie. "It's getting across the water that worries me. We haven't found a reliable captain yet. It's already an untenable situation in Italy, and if Germany continues along their path, we will need more help."

Ben agreed but pushed aside his worry to offer comfort. He took Agnes's aged hands in his roughed ones. "You always tell me to trust the good Lord. His eye is on the sparrow so that He will provide a way." He must.

Children like Amalie were getting caught in the power struggle of angry men. He knew how that felt, albeit on a much smaller scale.

A knock at the door caused a whimper from Amalie. Agnes shooed Ben over to shield the child from whoever was at the door. As much as Benjamin wanted to be the one to answer, Agnes, at her age, disarmed everyone without resorting to the type of violence Ben was too often forced to use.

"Telegram, Miss Blair." Callum, the telegraph operator's teen-aged son, handed Agnes the paper. "Need to reply?"

Agnes scanned the paper. "No, but thank you. You have a fine day now."

As she paid the lad and closed the door, her cautious movement made the hair stand up on the back of Ben's neck. "What is it?"

She glanced at Amalie, who watched them with wide blue eyes.

"You need to get to Otto." Agnes tore the telegraph into small bits.

"Herr Otto?" Amalie's jaw quivered. "Da's friend?"

Agnes nodded. "There's a rumor the German Student Union plans to burn books that do not agree with the Nazi party politics."

Ben's gut twisted. He'd tried to get Otto to leave when he rescued Amalie. The Jewish man owned the bookstore frequented by students of the university where Amalie's father had worked. He was also a hub for sending information out of Germany. However, since he was also outspoken against the party, he would surely be one of the specific targets of such an event.

"Max, too?" Amalie tugged Ben's shirt.

He glanced at Agnes as he knelt, but she had no more information than he. "Who is Max, Amalie?" Otto was unmarried and had no children.

"Herr Otto is Max's new da." Amalia abandoned English as tears slipped down her cheeks. "His father left him with Otto a week before you brought me here. Max is a baby, but he looks funny. He won't have anyone to care for him if you don't bring him here. Please, Mr. Ben. Please. You have to save Max."

Ben wrapped Amalie in a hug as she sobbed. He wouldn't be sick. He wouldn't let this wee one see his anger. Once he wrestled it down, he cupped her small shoulders in his large hands and stared her in the eye. "I'm going right now, and I will do everything I can to bring Max here."

Amalie sniffed and nodded. "You come back, too."

Ben kissed her forehead, then stood. Agnes pressed a sack of provisions into his hand. "Godspeed, Benjamin."

Without a word, he left the house and broke into a jog. He would never arrive in time if the bonfires started tomorrow. *Keep Otto and Max safe.* He supposed it was a prayer, not that God listened to the likes of him. But for an innocent child, surely God would hear such a plea, even from a guilty man like himself.

Chapter Four

WEDNESDAY, MAY 17, 1933

"So this is where he's been?" Eleanor stepped from the train at the Fort Augustus Railway Station, Hiram behind her.

"Not quite like home," the older man muttered. He'd been an excellent companion, just like Eleanor knew he would be. Quiet, unassuming, but protective.

Eleanor shivered at the damp air. "Surely it's no warmer here than at home, but this chill gets in the bones."

Hiram grunted. "Let's get your trunk."

This time, Eleanor followed Hiram. A handful of passengers disembarked with them, but all scurried on their way without stopping at the luggage car. She passed Hiram and the stationmaster before coming to the end of the platform.

Beyond was a large body of vibrant blue water stretching toward the horizon. On either side, cliffs rose. They were not nearly as high as the mountains of home, but their jaggedness reminded her of the foothills outside Blue Spruce. Mist stretched long fingers down the green crags. Perhaps the hills were higher than she thought?

"Eleanor," Hiram called.

While she'd been woolgathering, he'd secured a wagon and loaded her small trunk and their two carpetbags in the bed. She placed her hand in his gnarled one as he aided her climb to the seat. He gathered the reins attached to a grey pony but hesitated.

"What is it?" She glanced over at him.

The man was near eighty, she guessed. No one knew exactly. His face was weathered like old leather, but green eyes sparked beneath bushy brows. Though he shaved each day, it seemed he had perpetual gray stubble along his jaw. Thin and wiry, he was stronger than he appeared and gentler than his reticent speech implied.

"We've come a long way." He stared ahead. "It's been sixteen years, Eleanor. Are you ready for who we'll find?"

Eleanor wrapped her shawl more tightly about her shoulders. "We have to try, Hiram. I don't know if he'll want to see me. I don't know if I'll be welcome. You will, of course."

"Don't sell yourself short, missy." He clucked to the horses. "That boy loved you once."

She blinked back the tears. "I loved him, too."

Probably still did. Or perhaps she was still in love with the memory of him. That's what scared her most right now. Hiram was right to ask his question. She wasn't ready to find out who Ben had become. If he wasn't the man—boy—she once knew …

Sixteen years.

The pony plodded out of Fort Augustus. Green grass spread along the plain. Creeks ran to or from the lake. Did they use the same terms here? She didn't know. She'd never left Montana before. Honestly, she'd never even been on a train.

Back in Blue Spruce, Silas and Hiram had bundled Eleanor on the train with as little fanfare as possible. No one to see her off, which hopefully meant George Brown didn't know she left, nor where she was headed. The gossips either. Though within a day, her absence would be noted. Sixteen years had passed, surely they wouldn't assume she'd gone in search of Ben.

Silas hadn't wanted to take the chance, however. Without much effort, people would learn she'd gone to New York, but he hoped that by delaying that knowledge by even a day, she could disappear into the crowds of that large city.

The wagon bumped beneath her as they crossed over a bridge. A small wooden sign declared they'd entered Bieldfell. Such an interesting name. She'd seen a lot of interesting town names as they traveled three days across the United States. Plains and fields and mountains and cities. Such variety all within the same country. It was truly a wonder.

And then New York City. She'd about panicked with so many people about. Crushing. Suffocating. She'd be happy to never visit that place again. Not that London was much better. But the ocean voyage? That was her favorite part of the trip. Nothing but water for as far as the eye could see. Like the mountains at home that stretched up to the big sky above, the water stretched to the horizon. If only gentlemen hadn't tried to court her at every turn.

"This is the road." Hiram interrupted her rememberings. "Heather Wynd. Odd name."

They crossed another bridge, and her stomach tightened. "Cora said to call at number seven."

They passed number one, then two. Her gaze stayed pinned to the numbers, scarcely registering the variety of home structures that lined the curving road. Large ones, small ones. Hidden ones, adorable ones.

Oh, wait. "That's number seven." She pointed, and Hiram halted the wagon.

It was set back from the road and surrounded by various flowers, creating a beautiful palette like that of the summertime back home. Ben had never been interested in flowers. What if ... what if he'd married?

Her stomach turned. In the far back of her mind, she'd asked the question but hadn't wanted to consider it. Even though she doubted Ben would like to see her, she'd always pictured him unmarried. There was hope in that image. That perhaps they could be reconciled one day. She would never marry, not after what happened. But if he had married another …

"I don't feel so good." She pressed a hand to her stomach. The food here in England or Scotland, or whatever country they'd come to, was so different. Why had Ben come to live here? Suddenly, all she wanted to do was turn around and go home.

"Come on, girlie." Hiram helped her down from the wagon. "Buck up. We've come this far, we've got to see it through."

Eleanor placed one foot in front of the other, mainly because Hiram had a firm hold of her arm and wouldn't let her stop moving forward. They reached the door, and Hiram knocked. A squeal sounded inside. Then a baby cried.

"I can't do this." Eleanor couldn't stop the tears. Ben had married. He had a family. All the humiliation she'd experienced back home. The gossips' snide comments. Mr. Brown's not-so-subtle attempts at making her life miserable. She'd been an outcast. Yet here she was about to meet Ben's … wife.

The door opened before she could free her arm from Hiram's grasp.

"Oh, hello." The older lady cocked her head. "Who might you be?"

Hiram cleared his throat. "This here's Eleanor—"

"May the Lord be praised." The woman's eyes turned to water, and she pulled Eleanor into an embrace. "You've come."

Eleanor froze, arms pinned at her sides. This wasn't the welcome she expected. Even when she dreamed of Ben being overjoyed at seeing her again, being embraced by an older lady who seemed to think Eleanor an answer to her prayers had never entered her wildest imagining.

"Who is it, Miss Agnes?" A small voice asked from within the cottage.

"Pardon me." Miss Agnes—apparently—sniffed as she released Eleanor. "I'm Agnes Blair. This is my home. Please, please come inside."

"Who are you?" A small girl with blonde braids and crystal blue eyes stared up at Eleanor. She looked nothing like Ben, with his black hair and darker skin tone.

"I'm Eleanor Finch." She pointed to her companion. "And that's Mr. Hiram. He's my friend."

"Like Miss Agnes is my friend?" the little girl asked.

Miss Agnes patted the little girl's head, though her smile quivered. "This is Amalie. And you hear baby Max awaking from his nap. I am so overjoyed to meet you. Sit at the table. I just made biscuits. Let me get Max, then I'll dish them up. You must be exhausted from your travels." She spun and disappeared through the only other door in the room.

Dumbfounded, Eleanor startled at the quiet whistle behind her. She spun around to find Hiram's face had turned a brilliant shade of red.

"What?" He yanked out a kitchen chair and sat with a huff. "I might be old, but I got eyes. She's a fine lookin' woman."

A laugh jumped from Eleanor's throat. This wasn't just another country. This was an entirely different world.

"I like your dress." Little Amalie touched the cotton fabric. She spoke slowly, with an odd accent. Eleanor had met enough members of the Blackfeet nation to recognize when English wasn't a first language, but this wasn't like their speech.

"Sit, sit." Miss Agnes bustled back with a baby in her arms. The child wasn't near as old as Cora's little one. "You must be exhausted from your journey."

Was this their contact? The one who told Cora about Ben? It would explain why she seemed to know more about them than they knew about … anything.

Heavy steps preceded the opening of the front door and a voice Eleanor could still hear in her dreams. "Agnes, why is the stationmaster's pony hitched at the front gate?"

Eleanor turned to face the giant of a man who looked nothing like the boy who had saved her life. "Ben?"

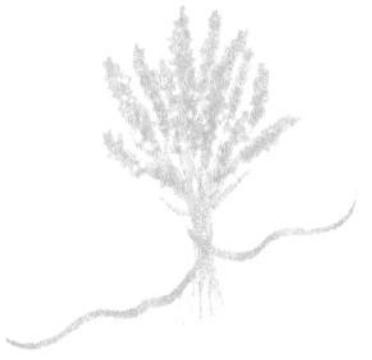

Chapter Five

"ELEANOR?" BEN STARED AT the woman standing in the middle of Agnes's home. Her name croaked from his throat. He tugged at his collar, but it didn't stop the suffocating feeling pressing on his lungs.

Suddenly aware that Agnes and Amalie watched him, he sucked in a gulp of air, then noticed the man sitting at Agnes's table.

"Hiram?" The man had been more of a father to him than the monster who sired him.

"You grew up, son." Hiram crossed his arms. "And you're not dead."

"Hiram." Eleanor hissed. But she offered no more words.

Not that he knew what to say either. She looked good, though she'd also grown up. Light hair pinned up in a woman's style. Curves he didn't recall from his boyish years, though he'd once thought to spend the rest of his life with her. What did he know of that at the age of eighteen? Just that she was his best friend.

Until he became a killer.

"You shouldn't be here." He spun toward the door, unwilling to reopen the old wound or reawaken the old longings. Reality slammed into him. "But you can't leave tonight. I'll bring your things to the porch, then return the wagon to the station."

Anything to get away, to keep Eleanor from seeing the man he'd become. He'd left to protect her from association with him, especially when Mr. Brown threatened to prosecute him, or lynch him if the court decided against it. Ben hadn't waited around to find out.

Then he'd settled in Beildfell of all places. *Bield* meant haven or safe place. His hut, Agnes's home, his work, had become that for him. Now Eleanor was here in his sanctuary.

A quiet step sounded behind him. He expected someone to follow him outside, one of the adults of course, not Amalie. Slowing his pace, he let the little girl catch up to him.

"Who is she?" Amalie asked in German. When he didn't answer right away, she continued, "Can I help you?"

He chuckled despite the grumpy angst in his chest. "An old friend, and yes, you may. Can you carry this carpet bag?" He handed her the old leather one he presumed to be Hiram's.

Amalie tottered as she half-dragged it to the porch. Ben lifted the trunk to his shoulder like a ship barrel. He held it in place with one hand and snatched the floral carpet bag with the other, then followed Amalie to the porch. He refused to return inside, not until he buried these feelings swirling in his chest.

"Coming to town with me?" He chucked Amalie under the chin. She grinned and grabbed his hand. As much as he wanted to be alone, the little girl's company soothed the raw places Eleanor's unexpected appearance created.

He would apologize for his abrupt departure later. Not that he owed her one. She'd surprised him, and he hated surprises. Working in intelligence took meticulous planning. Yes, things went awry, but those situations were met with contingencies and with a certain expectation of things going wrong. Eleanor's presence? Never in his dreams had he pictured her appearing here in Bieldfell.

"What's her name?" Amalie asked as he lifted her onto the wagon seat.

He climbed up beside her and urged the pony into motion, not wanting to admit that he didn't know whether Eleanor was still *Miss* Finch or whether she'd married. He always assumed she had, but why would a married woman travel across an ocean to find him? His heart stuttered, and he almost turned the pony around. What if she brought news that his grandparents had died?

"She's pretty." Amalie shrugged, then launched into tales of Max's antics, which reminded him of the reason he'd stopped by Agnes's house. He had news about Otto.

The man lost his entire bookshop during the book burnings, and it had taken Ben nearly forty-eight hours to make sure he was still alive. He was, but insisted on staying behind for a reason he wouldn't tell Ben. So Ben had brought Max to Agnes until Otto could get out of Germany. *If* he could get out of Germany. At last message, he'd made it as far as the underground stop in Düsseldorf, hopefully headed for the border of The Netherlands, a companion in tow. It was the companion part that worried Ben. Something warned him it was a woman but Otto didn't have a girlfriend or fiancée.

"Why weren't you happy to see Eleanor?" Amalie's question jarred Ben back to the moment. Fortunately, they had just reached the train station, which allowed Ben an excuse not to answer the little girl's question. Besides, it was a complicated one. It thrilled, hurt, and worried him to see Eleanor again.

He stopped the wagon near the station and helped Amalie down as the stationmaster appeared. "Morning, sir. Returning your pony." He handed over the reins.

"Ah, that pretty lady and the old gent didn't have a mind to return them?" The question was more curious than critical.

"I like her. I want her to stay," Amalie added in English, her chin tilted so she could converse with the men.

"They're visiting Agnes." Ben tugged her braid. "Not every day we get strangers staying in town." Not that Eleanor and Hiram were strangers exactly.

The stationmaster patted his pony's shoulder. "Then the third stranger didn't accompany them?"

Ben forced himself not to react. "Third stranger? Haven't seen anyone else new around." And in a small town, every newcomer stood out.

The stationmaster rubbed his chin. "Dressed like the older gent. Those worn blue trousers."

"Denim jeans," Ben muttered. He hadn't worn them in ages but missed their durable quality.

"Had a swagger like you. Beard, too." The man speared Ben with a serious gaze. "Not sure I liked the look of him. He kept a close eye on the lady as if he were aiming to speak with her, but not when her chaperone was present. Be honest, I didn't like it."

Ben's nerves stood on end. A skill he'd honed first as a youth to stay free of his father's fists and then out on the range when the wolves started howling. It served him well as they built the underground, but he'd never had cause to need those instincts around Fort Augustus. The most dangerous thing they faced was mudslides or the annoyance of ticks and midges. He could rest here, which is why he'd made it his home.

"Thanks for the information, I'll share it with Hiram." Ben purposefully used the man's name so the stationmaster would consider him a neighbor to be trusted. "You have a good day. C'mon, Amalie, let's get back to Agnes."

"Do you think that stranger wants to talk to Miss Eleanor?" Amalie switched to German as she skipped to keep up with Ben. Usually, he'd slow down so she could keep up, but this news drove him to return to Eleanor as quickly as possible.

"Your English is improving."

"I understand it because Agnes speaks it so much." Amalie fell silent, and just as he hoped that would be the end of her questions about Eleanor, she again asked, "Why weren't you happy to see Eleanor? You're worried now."

He sighed but adjusted his hold on her hand so she knew his disquiet had nothing to do with her. "Eleanor and I were children together. Then something bad happened, and I had to leave. I haven't seen her in sixteen years."

Amalie's eyes widened. "That's a long time."

They crossed the bridge leading out of Fort Augustus. "Yes, a lifetime." Memories flooded him. Good memories. Wonderful memories. Until—

"Why did she stay away so long?"

"It's not that she stayed away." She should have. Had danger followed her from Montana, or had she picked up a thug on this side of the ocean? "I did."

"Oh?" Amalie frowned. "You have always lived in Bieldfell, haven't you?"

Ben shook his head. "I used to live in a place called Montana, in America."

She tilted her head, her blonde braids swinging. "That's far away."

"Uh-huh. Across an ocean."

"She swam all that way?"

Ben smiled despite his worry. "No, she took a boat, just like we did to come here. England and Scotland are an island. It takes a boat to reach us no matter which country you come from."

Amalie was silent for a moment while she considered his words. "If she took a boat and came a long way like I did, why did you not say hello? You weren't very kind, Mr. Ben."

Leave it to a child to speak the truth and drive guilt deep into his gut. "You're right, Miss Amalie. I was a bear." But what else was new?

"When I did something my mom said was unkind, she told me I should say sorry. Will you say you're sorry? Miss Eleanor looks nice. I want her to stay, like I told the station man."

"I reckon you're right." He swallowed, knowing precisely what else Amalie's parents would suggest, that he ask God for pardon, too.

He tilted his head back to look at the overcast sky. He knew clouds could not hide him from God or hide God from him, but at the moment, they felt like an iron shield. Or perhaps that was merely his conscience. Yet God felt as far away as home.

Except home had found him here.

Heaven help him ... if he had to protect her again, he wouldn't hesitate to use whatever force necessary to save her life. Again.

Chapter Six

ELEANOR PACED THE SMALL cottage. Though tired from travel, she couldn't sit, not when Ben had taken one look at her and ran.

Hiram nursed a cup of coffee, fortunately keeping his opinion to himself. She didn't need him telling her what she should do about Ben. Not that she knew *what* she should do next.

Agnes sat at the table helping the baby drink from a cup, spilling more down the outside of him than inside. Yet the determined expression warned she also didn't want to be told what to do.

The child, Max, wasn't as old as Cora's baby, Eleanor was pretty sure, but he also didn't look like her friend's little boy. Baby Max had a shock of thin blonde hair that stood on end and eyes a shape she'd not seen before. They were almost oval-shaped and made him appear tired with little bags under his wide blue eyes. Yet he sported the biggest grin when he should be cranky since Agnes's attempt at feeding him wasn't going to plan.

"Why didn't Otto send this child with a bottle?" Agnes huffed. "How did Ben feed this poor baby? This isn't working."

"Took you long enough to figure that out," Hiram muttered.

Before Eleanor could scold, Agnes raised a brow. "If you want to try, old man, be my guest."

"Seeing as I already am, hand me the babe." Hiriam reached across the table. Max giggled as he was passed from one to the other. "Now, got any soda pop bottles?"

"You're not giving him that!" Agnes glared at Hiram.

"Of course not, old woman." Hiram glared right back. "Pour it in a cup. *I'll* drink the soda. Then, pour the babe's milk into the bottle. We'll put a cloth over it, and he can suck the milk without it pouring down his chest."

"Where'd you learn that?" Agnes asked as she followed his direction.

"Cora always makes sure she has soda on hand." Eleanor offered, though she'd never seen her friend use it in such a way.

"It's a last resort when a calf won't take its mama's milk, another cow won't take the calf, and the usual bottles are unavailable." He set the cloth-clovered bottle opening to Max's little mouth. "Necessity breeds creativity."

"I still wonder how Ben fed the little man." Agnes tapped her chin. "Poor thing didn't come with much other than the clothes on his back. I thought to borrow a bottle, but no one has a free one and everyone has an opinion."

Eleanor could relate to that. "Where is Max's mother?" Was the child Ben's?

Agnes glanced at Eleanor as if she weighed Eleanor's character. It made Eleanor squirm, but she tried to stand up to the scrutiny. She'd had enough of it over the years.

"Wouldn't Ben have the materials to care for his son?" All right, so she was digging for questions and not standing up to Agnes's search as well as she wished, but they traveled halfway around the world in search of Ben, and the man disappeared. "And what about the little girl? Is she his, too?"

Agnes smiled and patted the table. "Sit, child. Our Ben is not married, nor does he have a girl or children. Max and Amalie are little ones he rescued from harm. They're staying here until we can find a new home for them."

Eleanor sank into the chair. She glanced at Hiram, who kept his focus on the baby, though she had no doubt he listened intently. "So Ben is still the man I knew. Protecting the innocent."

"He doesn't think so." Agnes rose, poured a cup of coffee and set the cup in front of Eleanor.

Clarity dawned. "Wait, you're the one who sent for us, aren't you?"

Agnes retook her seat. "I am. I believe we each have friends who know one another. Or knew a mutual friend. I'm not entirely sure, only that I trusted my friend to get a message to you."

"To me? Not Ben's grandparents?" Again, Eleanor glanced at Hiram. Did he understand any of this?

"I have my reasons, child." Agnes smiled. "And you, Hiram, have a grandfather's touch."

Hiram grunted. "I ain't never married, nor sired a kid to have grandchildren."

Except Ben had been like a son to him. Eleanor kept that information to herself. "Did Ben know you told us where to find him?" She guessed not.

"Och, no." Agnes laughed. "You saw his reaction. Had I warned him, I feared he might flee the island.

Amalie's chatter preceded her entrance, Ben close on her heels. He shut the door as soon as they cleared it, his gaze immediately going to Eleanor. Eleanor tightened her grip on the edge of her chair in an attempt to stay seated, but the intensity of his eyes speared straight through her. Who was this man who used to be her best friend?

"Everything all right?" Hiram obviously noted Ben's ... Eleanor didn't even know what to call this ... this ...

"Three strangers got off the train." Amalie tucked herself under Agnes's arm, the child's accent thickening her words.

"Three?" Agnes prompted the girl to continue.

"Uh-huh." Amalie nodded, then counted on her fingers. "Mr. Hiram, Miss Eleanor, and someone else. Ben did not like that."

Eleanor's gaze connected with Hiram. Had someone followed them here? Silas knew Mr. Brown would begin searching for her as soon as he realized she was gone, but they hoped the chaos of New York would shield them. Had they been wrong?

"Is it someone we should watch out for?" Agnes asked Ben as she tugged the little girl closer.

"Yes." Ben's voice had deepened in the last sixteen years, yet it sent an odd electricity straight to Eleanor's toes. "Keep the children inside until we know more."

"You got a spare weapon on hand?" Hiram set down the bottle and rocked the sleeping Max in the crook of his arm. "I'll keep an eye on the children and the lady."

Agnes snorted. "First, I can care for the children just fine without you, sir. Second, I have a hunting rifle up high on a shelf where the children can't reach it. I don't need your gunslinging ways in my home."

"Gunslinging?" Hiram laughed. "Ma'am, I've had to protect calves from bears, cougars, and wolves more times than I've hair on my head. Ya don't need to aim at a beast to scar 'im off."

"Precisely." Agnes raised her chin. "And I can aim at the sky just as well as you can."

"Eleanor?" Ben's whisper pulled her away from the verbal sparring. He cocked his head toward the door and left without another word.

As much as Eleanor wouldn't mind seeing who won this particular match, she slipped outside after Ben. Her heart pounded. This would be their first conversation in sixteen years, and now she had no idea what to say.

Ben stood on the walk, hands braced on his hips. The damp air caused a shiver to run through Eleanor and she tightened her shawl.

"Did you not bring a coat?" Ben asked over his shoulder.

The man had eyes in the back of his head. "It's in my bag here because it was uncomfortable to wear on the train." Why did she feel the need to defend herself?

"Why have you come, Eleanor?" Ben's question was quieter than his first. "Are my grandparents all right? My aunts and cousins, too?"

"They are all still alive, if that's what you want to know." Eek, that was none too nice a tone lacing her words. "I'm sorry, Ben. You've been missed."

"If you do not bring bad news ..." He turned to face her, dark eyes boring into her, rooting her to the spot. "I'll ask again, Eleanor. Why have you come?"

This time, the shiver was not due to the cold air, nor could she move to fetch her coat. Her body trembled under the coldness in Ben's expression. This wasn't the same boy who had been her friend. He'd grown up, yes. Taller, broader, but darker, too. Not just his hair and skin. Even his eyes had lost their light. The tattoos that peeked out from his collar and sleeves hinted at a life lived with the underbelly of society.

"I came to bring my friend home." Tears pricked her eyes and caught in her throat. "But I'm not sure I found him."

"You're right." Even his tone was dark and cold. "The boy you knew died that day. I'll pay your passage home. It's not safe for you to remain here."

Her trembling legs gave out, and she sank to sit atop her trunk. "Not safe because of you or because of the stranger that might have followed me?"

"Both." His jaw jumped beneath his beard. She would have missed it if she hadn't been sitting, forcing her to look up at him. "Eleanor, what do you want from me?"

A sob was her only response. She covered her face, heard the door open, but it wasn't Ben's hand on her shoulder, it was Agnes at her side.

"Come, child." The woman wrapped a blanket around her shoulders and tugged her to her feet. "You've had a long journey, and this conversation will be better in the morning."

Even though he'd broken her heart anew, Eleanor looked her watery gaze. "Goodnight, Ben."

Agnes didn't let her wait for a reply.

Chapter Seven

BEN SAT AMONGST THE sheep that grazed near the hut he called home. It sat partway up the hill directly to the west of Loch Ness, and without the usual haze and mist, he had a clear view down to the water.

Not that he could see it in the dark. It sat like a dark slash in the night.

The sheep rustled and Ben caught the quiet pad of footsteps. "Come to keep watch, Hiram?"

The older man chuckled. "Your awareness has improved."

"Hard to miss a cattleman's ability to keep animals calm, whether they know him or not." Ben leaned back on his elbows. "You sure the girls are safe with the two of us up here?"

Hiram grunted as he lowered himself to the cold ground. "Agnes is quite capable."

"You find it amusing to rile her." Ben stared at his friend. He never knew the man to have a wife or girl or any interest in a female. Until this afternoon.

"Get it outta yer head, boy." Hiram matched Ben's position, bringing back memories of cattle drives, sitting together under the stars in the wide open spaces back in Montana.

He let his head fall back. No stars tonight. It's the one thing he didn't like about Scotland. "Do you think she'll forgive me?"

"I reckon." Hiram sighed. "She expected you to be happy to see her. Aren't you?"

Ben snorted. "It's been sixteen years."

"What's that gotta do with anything?"

"Look at me, Hiram. I've turned into my father. Eleanor doesn't need to have anything to do with me."

Hiram studied him a moment. "Are you sure you haven't turned into your grandfather?"

"A beast or a monster. What's the difference?"

Hiram swore under his breath, causing Ben to sit up. The old man never used such language and would punish cowboys who said such things around his employer's grandkids.

"Obviously *you* think there's a difference," Ben challenged.

"I know your father used his fists." Hiram met his gaze. "You ever see your grandfather use his?"

"No. But I have."

"On an innocent person?"

Ben looked away. "I've killed, Hiram. It does things to a man's soul."

"You think your grandfather doesn't know that? The man served in the Union army. It took the love of a good woman to show him the way out of the darkness."

"Waxing poetic in your old age."

Hiram shoved his shoulder, barely causing Ben to sway. "You need taking down a notch, kid. Right full of yourself."

"I never claimed to be a saint." Ben pulled up his knees and rested his forearms on them. "Quite the opposite, actually."

"If you want to wallow in your self-pity, fine." Hiram pushed to his feet. "Brood out here all you want, but there's a good woman down there who sees you as a hero. Don't hurt her."

"Why do you think I've stayed away for sixteen years? It's been torture not to see her, to know she's moved on."

"She hasn't, Ben." Hiram crossed his arms. "Brown has made her life miserable. She's a shell of herself. No family, hardly any friends. She got the news you were here and could leave within hours, leaving nothing behind. If you reject her right now, you will hurt her far worse than anyone else could."

Ben absorbed the news. Stunned. "Why?"

"Why would your rejection hurt?"

"No, I get that now." Ben scrubbed his face. "She's the sweetest soul on earth. Why wouldn't she have family and friends?"

"Because Brown spread lies about her and the busybodies destroyed her reputation." Hiram returned to sit beside him. "You weren't the only one whose life was ruined that day, Ben. Hers was, too. And then you left and let her take the repercussions alone."

Deep, horrible pain welled inside of him. He tucked his chin, hiding his head beneath his arms. "I'm a monster, Hiram."

"She doesn't think so." Hiram bumped his shoulder. "And neither does that other little girl. She sang your praises until Agnes finally convinced her to sleep."

A smile tugged at his mouth.

"You know, this place has a couple similarities to home."

Ben grinned. "They're hills, Hiram. Ain't nothing like the mountains."

"Phshaw, of course not." Hiram leaned back on his palms. "Maybe a few foothills. The ruggedness. Animals grazing. Lakes."

"Here they're called lochs."

"Eh, sounds the same." Hiram paused. "You doing all right, son?"

Ben returned his arms to his knees and stared out at Loch Ness. "I'm making a difference. I can't save them all, but I've rescued several children the last year or so. I fear another war is on the horizon."

"We haven't heard anything about no war. Back home, it's been hard enough to feed a family. Lots of people out of work and the drought ..." Hiram sighed. "We have a new president who is making all these new deals, trying to reassure everyone with his fancy fireside chats on the radio. Don't know that it'll work, but it sure can't get worse."

What could a man say to that? "You should get some sleep, Hiram. You traveled half way around the world."

"You calling me old?" Hiram grunted.

"If the shoe fits." Ben grinned and ducked away from Hiram's half-hearted backhanded slap. "Honest, though. It's good to see you."

"You come to breakfast and take that little lady out for a stroll, yeah?" Hiram stood again. "I'll keep my eye out for that stranger the stationmaster mentioned, but you watch your back."

"I always do."

Ben stayed outside for a few more hours before his body convinced him to get a few hours of shuteye. On his way to Agnes's house, he detoured to Fort Augustus to check for any new telegrams. With his reclusive and often-absent behavior, they held his telegrams until he called for them.

The Home Office, or US intelligence, always delivered the coded messages via Agnes.

Another message from Otto waited for him. Why the man insisted on messaging Ben directly, albeit in code, when he could communicate through official channels, Ben didn't know. It worried him, honestly. His instincts warned that something wasn't right about the whole situation.

Oh, he didn't worry about Otto's integrity or that he'd been compromised. Quite the opposite. The man fully embraced the resistance and would willingly sacrifice his life for it. His bookstore had been a place for the resistance to gather, a place to disseminate coded messages. And he took in Max, who appeared to have Down Syndrome. The child would be marked just as much as someone with Jewish heritage.

He opened the telegraph as he walked toward Agnes's house. Apparently, Otto now had two companions. No mention of whether he'd made it out of Germany yet, but Ben doubted it. How many people would the man rescue on his way out of the country?

Ben couldn't be frustrated with him. Leaving the country meant helping from afar, which is why Ben wouldn't give up helping the cause. Only, for him, the danger meant nothing. He did not look German, no, but his dark qualities helped him blend into the shadows. He had no physical deformities and no Jewish blood. He looked like a thug and, most of the time, that meant people left him alone.

He tucked the message away as he turned onto Heather Wynd. During the fall, the heather in the area spread purple up and down the highlands. It always reminded him of Eleanor, her soft, sweet nature. Her willingness to follow him on adventures and her trust in him when he got them into a scrape. He'd missed his friend and regret stabbed deep.

As he approached Agnes's cottage, the front door opened, framing Eleanor. Surprise lit her face, then apprehension stole the light. He'd done that.

"Ellie." The old nickname slipped out, softening the hardness in her shoulders. He swallowed. He could kill with his bare hands if it meant saving an innocent. But offering an apology to the girl who still held what was left of his heart? Oh yeah, he was nothing but a yellow-bellied coward.

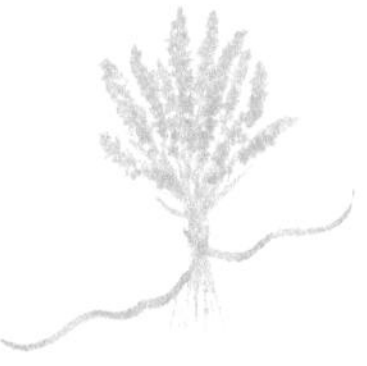

Chapter Eight

ELEANOR BLINKED, STUNNED AT the fear she saw in Ben's eyes. He didn't shutter it away from her, either.

Hearing Amalie's voice inside, followed by Max's cry, she quickly closed the door, leaving her and Ben alone in front of the cottage. The movement closed the space between them so that she had to look up. His beard was bushier than she realized. Coarse and curly and black. And long. He looked like a mountain man instead of the cowboy she remembered.

His throat bobbed beneath his beard. "I'm sorry, El."

That brought her eyes all the way up to his brown ones. So dark, they were almost black. Once upon a time, they'd twinkled with good humor. Then Georgie Brown attacked her. She turned away from Ben and shivered.

"You're cold." Ben gently rested his coat over her shoulders. Its warmth enveloped her, and she found herself leaning toward her old friend. His hands caught her upper arms, keeping distance between them.

"I missed you," she whispered.

"I'm no good for you, El." He bent forward, his forehead resting atop her head. "I will only cause you pain."

"I don't believe that." She spun too quickly, finding herself an inch from Ben's face. She sucked in a breath, but couldn't move. He'd only kissed her twice. Once before Georgie's attack and again the night before he disappeared. If only she'd known that was a goodbye kiss. In the years since, she savored it. To find him that close again? Dizziness made her sway.

"Careful." He wrapped his arms around her, holding her against his chest. "I don't want to hurt you."

Words stayed trapped in her throat. She didn't care who saw them or what the gossips in this little Scottish town said … She'd found Ben, and he held her as if no time had passed.

"Let's get inside." Ben's words were rough, and he set her away from him. He was right, of course. Such a display would do neither of them any good. But she couldn't be sorry for it. Not after she'd wished for that embrace for sixteen years.

Both Hiram and Agnes gave Ben, not Eleanor, a skeptical look when they reentered the house. Amalie, however, raced into Ben's legs. "Good morning!"

"Hey, good English, frauline." Ben tugged on the girl's braid. He glanced at Eleanor. "Amalie is learning English. She's only been at it for a short time, but she's picking it up faster than I learned German."

"You know German?" Eleanor tried not to gape. But Ben? Know another language?

The skin above his beard pinked. "French, Italian, too, and picking up more. Turns out I have a knack for languages."

Would wonders never cease? "That's amazing, Ben."

"You think so?" He studied her expression as if craving her approval.

"Absolutely." She felt Hiram, who was feeding Max his makeshift bottle, and Agnes watching them closely. "You could always communicate well with the friends who would visit your grandfather from the reservation."

"What's a rez-er-cation?" Amalie looked up at them from where she leaned against Ben's leg.

"*Reservation*. Well, it's ..." Ben placed his large hand on Amalie's head and sighed, then switched to a language Eleanor didn't recognize. Hiram scowled, but Agnes sighed and shifted the kettle to a warmer spot on the stove.

Amalie's eyes widened as Ben spoke, then she planted her fists on her hips and glared at Eleanor. "That is wrong." Then she stomped to Agnes who hugged her, an expression of sympathy on her face.

"What is wrong?" Eleanor looked to Ben for help. Had she done something that hurt the child? Hiram shrugged.

Ben shoved his hands into his pockets. "Amalie is Jewish, and because of that, she can no longer attend school in Germany. I explained that the US government forced members of the Blackfoot tribe to give up their land to live in a certain area. She understands how hurtful it is and, since you're from America, she connected you to her pain."

"Oh, poor thing." Eleanor's heart broke. What could she say? She had nothing to do with the harm her government had caused, nor did she know anything about what was happening in Germany, but she could feel Amalie's pain. The ache of being ostracized because of *who* she was and what someone else had done to her.

Amalie's gaze connected with Eleanor. "You, too?"

The other adults in the room froze, but Eleanor nodded and knelt. "Not because I'm Jewish or because I'm a member of the Blackfoot, but because people assumed something bad about me that didn't happen."

Amalie pulled away from Agnes, her blonde brows scrunched together. "Why do they think that?"

"I wish I knew, Amalie." Eleanor sighed. She kept the rest of her thoughts to herself. Ben had saved her life, yes, but now that Eleanor saw what he'd done for Amalie, a deep ache bloomed and she wished Ben had taken her with him when he fled Blue Spruce.

Amalie darted across the floor, flinging her arms around Eleanor's neck. Eleanor hugged the child. A bond had formed between them and for the first time in sixteen years, she felt like someone saw the deepest pain in her heart. The innocence of this child soothed the wound and Eleanor prayed she could show Amalie the same love.

"Breakfast will be ready soon." Agnes broke the spell. "Sit yourselves at the table."

"If that bacon tastes half as good as it smells, I hope you made enough." Hiram set the bottle on the table and lifted Max to his shoulder.

"There's sausage and scones to fill that belly of yours, Hiram." Agnes poured the heated water into a teapot. "I hope you like eggs, too."

Hiram's eyes lit up. "This is my kind of meal."

Eleanor shared a smile with Ben as he held out a seat for her beside Hiram. Amalie slid into the chair beside hers. Ben sat on the other side. As Agnes set the steaming meat, the warm scones, and the teapot on the table, Eleanor had this abiding sense that she'd come home. It was a feeling she hadn't experienced in a long, long time. Since before her mother died. No, probably since before her father died, when she was about Amalie's age.

"Ben, bless this food." Agnes sat and held her hands out to either side. Hiram held Max in his right arm, so Eleanor could only take Amalie's little hand.

"Almighty God, Father of all mercies." Reverence filled Ben's voice as he prayed. "We thine unworthy servants do give thee most humble and hearty thanks for all thy goodness and loving-kindness to us and to all men. Amen."

A warm hum followed as plates were passed, compliments made, and the food devoured. Hiram and Agnes bickered, but Hiram refused to give up holding Max. Amalie chattered about what made the Scottish Highlands different from her home in Germany. And Ben stayed silent, though Eleanor couldn't stop casting glances at him.

"Tell me about your travel here." Agnes pulled Eleanor's attention with a teasing glint in her eye. Hiram raised his brows, and Eleanor felt heat rise in her cheeks.

"You rode on a boat?" Amalie asked before stuffing a huge bite of scone in her mouth.

"First, a train." Eleanor smiled at her. "Then a boat. It took five days to get all the way across the ocean."

"Both were uneventful?" Ben glanced between her and Hiram, the undercurrent of his question clear.

"It was all out of the ordinary." Eleanor slid her eggs around her plate, remembering how overwhelming the trip had been. Miles upon miles of landscape she'd never seen before. Then the assault on her senses that day in New York City, only to finally be aboard a ship filled with so many different people. "Your grandparents were kind, Ben. They funded a second-class ticket for us."

"Wish you would have stayed in the cabin." Hiram finished off his bacon. "I had a time of it fending off those would-be suitors."

Eleanor kept her gaze on her plate, afraid of what Ben and Agnes might be thinking of her.

"Stay in a room for days?" Amalie came to her rescue with the most adorable expression of disgust.

"Any men give you a particularly hard time?" Ben asked.

"No, not that I noticed." Hiram sipped his tea with a grimace. "Any chance ya got some coffee here?"

"Don't be uncivilized." Agnes glared at him. "I cooked for you, didn't I?"

"It was right fine, woman, but a man needs his coffee."

Eleanor bit her lip to keep from laughing, Ben covered his face with his hand, and Amalie cocked her head in confusion.

"If you want coffee, then order some yourself." Agnes grabbed the teapot and refilled her cup.

"How about if I order some today?" Ben offered. "I want to have a listen around Bieldfell to see if I can track down news of the stranger who disembarked the train with you."

"I should come with you." Eleanor set down her fork. As delicious as the food was, she didn't have much appetite. "If he was one of the men who tried to speak with me on the ship, I'd recognize him."

"It's not safe, El." Ben rose. "I'm going alone."

"Girl's got a point, son." Hiram wiped his grizzled chin with a cloth napkin. "And if she's with you, she'll be safe enough."

"I want to go to town." Amalie bounced.

"You have lessons, young lady." Agnes shook her finger. "Just because the German government won't let you attend school, that doesn't apply here. Education is important, especially nowadays."

Amalie pouted.

"I'm sure you could show me a thing or two about sums." Hiram shifted the sleeping baby to the other arm. "Besides, Agnes might try to poison me with more of that tea stuff. You'll protect me, right?"

Amalie grinned, and Hiram winked.

"He's an old coot," Agnes rolled her eyes, "but he has a point. You two need to talk, so get on with you."

Eleanor looked to Ben, hoping he wouldn't welcome her begrudgingly. She hadn't seen him in sixteen years. Whether it was forward or not, she'd traveled halfway around the world to see him and didn't want to miss a minute.

Ben rubbed his neck—was it a little red?—and cast a glance at her. "All right. Get your coat. Mornings are chilly around here."

Eleanor grinned. She knew it wouldn't be like old times since they were adults and all, but how she wished it could be. She'd missed her friend.

Chapter Nine

THIS WAS A BAD idea. Ben closed the front door behind him as Eleanor led the way to the road. It felt too much like a ... what did young people call it today? Like he was courting her? Which he was most definitely not doing. Couldn't do. Wouldn't do.

"Do you walk everywhere?" Eleanor tugged gloves onto her hands as she waited for him to catch up.

"Distances are much shorter here than in Montana." He shoved his hands into his coat pockets to avoid taking hers.

"There, it made sense to saddle a horse to ride everywhere. Here, no need."

"What do you like most about Scotland?"

He started walking with a huff. "I know you're trying to be sociable, but do we need to do that?"

When she didn't reply, he glanced at her just as a tear slipped down her cheek.

"El." He sighed. "What did you hope for when you agreed to find me? That I'd throw open my arms to welcome you? That I'm the same boy I was before Brown tried to hang me for murder? I killed his son. I've killed since."

She pursed her lips, increasing her speed toward town.

"How do you think I got Amalie away from the officer who killed her parents? I had to kill him before he killed her. She is an innocent child. I couldn't let—"

"Of course, you couldn't let him harm her." Eleanor glared at him. "Do you think I don't know that? You did the same thing for me. And then you left."

"You didn't need to be connected to a killer, El."

"Did you even think I might be tainted because of that situation whether you left or not?" Eleanor shook her head and continued down the path. "You haven't asked me anything."

"What were you expecting, El?" He quickly caught up to her. "It's been sixteen years."

"Did you miss us?" Eleanor increased her pace as if she didn't really want to know the answer.

Perhaps if he let her walk far enough ahead of him, he wouldn't have to answer. They crossed the bridge over the creek that indicated the beginning of Heather Wynd. Eleanor slowed, though she didn't look at him.

"This way." He led them toward Bieldfell's town center. They marched along in tense silence. He knew he'd hurt her, but how could he get her to see that returning to their old friendship wasn't possible? *He* wasn't the boy who'd left.

"What's the name of that body of water?" Eleanor pointed.

"Loch Ness."

"Loch?" Eleanor cocked her head. "Sounds like a funny way to say *lake*."

"Up in the Highlands, the people have spoken Scottish Gaelic, likely with origins from Ireland from centuries ago."

"Do you know Scottish Gaelic?"

"*Beagan*."

"What?"

He stifled a grin. "Beagan. It means *a little*."

"You really do pick up languages, don't you?"

Ben shrugged. "I suppose so. It's important to be able to talk to someone in a language they understand."

Eleanor fell silent, and Ben wished he could guess what she was thinking. Before he could work up the nerve to ask, they reached the village. Neighbors gave him a wide berth as they usually did—he knew he had a frightening persona, just like his grandfather—but they also gave Eleanor curious glances.

She sidled closer to him, the first indication of her unease. As more and more of his neighbors openly showed their curiosity, she wrapped her arm around his. It did something to his insides. He'd missed her touch, but this was different. She never used to shy away from people. The Eleanor he remembered was adventurous, daring, and willing to travel to a whole different country to track down an old friend. This ... fear was not like her, and it ramped up his protective side.

He held the door to the grocers and he felt her take a huge inhale before she stepped into the dim interior. He followed, blinking as his eyes adjusted.

"Good morning." Mrs. Allan appeared from between two shelves. Her smile faded when she spotted Ben. She focused her attention on Eleanor. "How may I help you today?"

Eleanor glanced at Ben, then licked her lips. "Do you happen to have any coffee beans?"

Mrs. Allan's lips puckered. "You're visiting Bieldfell."

"Yes, ma'am." Eleanor again glanced at Ben. Thankfully, she didn't add more detail.

"Are you visiting ..." Mrs. Allan lowered her voice ... "*him?*"

"Who?" Eleanor looked mystified, bless her.

"She's an old friend who stopped by to see me with her grandfather." Ben boldly lied, but if it protected Eleanor, he'd let it sit on his conscience instead of hers. "They're on their way to a tour of the Continent."

"Ah." Mrs. Allan's expression cleared. "And your grandfather likes his coffee, I don't doubt."

"Yes, ma'am." Again, Eleanor glanced at Ben, clearly confused, but willing to go with the woman as she bustled down another aisle.

Ben waited by the counter, picking up a newspaper to look busy. Mrs. Allan didn't like him, he knew. Well, it wasn't that she *disliked* him. It was more that she didn't trust him. As she shouldn't, and Ben didn't take offense. However, he hadn't considered what the woman would think of Eleanor when she walked into the shop with him. Distancing himself from Eleanor, inserting the news of a grandfather chaperone, would protect Eleanor from gossip.

Which brought to mind what Eleanor had been trying to tell him on the walk over here. What she'd had to endure back in Blue Spruce. Had other shopkeepers treated her like Mrs. Allan? But why? Ben wasn't there to sully her reputation. They should have taken care of her, protected her from a shark like Brown. Especially after her mother passed away.

The bell above the door jangled as a customer walked in. Another lady who hesitated when she noticed Ben. He knew full well that his large stature, black beard, and tattoos scared these women, but they were useful tools when operating in the shadows of society. One had to look like the darkness in order to rescue the innocent.

"Good morning." Mrs. Allan waved at the newcomer. "I have the soap you ordered here behind the counter. Let me finish with this sweet girl first."

Ben backed up to give them more space and allow Mrs. Allan to think herself Eleanor's protector.

"Did you hear there was another sighting?" The other customer—Ben couldn't remember her name—hushed her voice.

"No." Mrs. Allan made change from the coins Eleanor had given her. "Was it Mrs. Mackay again?"

"Fishermen this time. They were sure they saw the monster."

"Monster?" Eleanor squeaked.

"Aye." Mrs. Allan handed her the small sack of coffee beans. "You'll want to be mindful if you go near the loch. There's a monster there that could eat a person, I've no doubt."

"Or capsize a boat." The other lady bobbed her head. "The fishermen were sure they wouldn't make it home."

"Monsters come in all shapes." Mrs. Allan patted Eleanor's wrist and cast a surreptitious glance at Ben.

"You're a visitor here, so you don't know them all. Stick close to your grandfather, eh?"

Eleanor opened her mouth, likely to protest, but Ben faked a cough. He pounded his chest and fled outside, hoping it would be enough to bring Eleanor hurrying after him. He didn't need her defending him or protesting. Ben had no problem with them thinking the truth about him. He was a killer, and that was monster enough.

He watched through the window as Eleanor pinned her lips closed. Lips he had no business staring at, so why was it so hard to look away? He scrubbed his face. Because he remembered their feel. He'd forced those memories away, but seeing Eleanor again brought them all back.

The door opened, and Eleanor waved at the ladies as she exited. "Thank you for the beans and the advice." He was surprised to see her shudder as she turned toward him.

"All clear?" Ben asked, when he really wanted to ask if she was okay. It'd been years, yes, but his activities meant honing his skill at spotting that nebulous *something* that warned when a situation was amiss. And whatever that was surrounded Eleanor like an invisible ring.

"I want to see the loch." Eleanor turned toward the body of water Ben had called Loch Ness and didn't wait for him as she hurried down the lane.

"We should get back to Agnes's house." Ben stayed by her side, his long legs easily keeping pace.

"No, we came to find information about that other stranger, and while you were scaring the ladies in the grocery, I have information."

Ben didn't hide his surprise.

Eleanor raised a brow. "Plus I want to see this lake with the monster. Is there really a monster, or is it a rumor?"

"I don't know." Ben's arm brushed hers as he slipped the bag of coffee beans from her hands, igniting more of those memories he'd forgotten. He shoved them back where they belonged. "People will keep looking at us if you walk with me. I should have thought of that earlier."

Eleanor wrapped her hand around his arm, bringing her close to his side. "I'm used to people looking at me like that. The difference, Ben, is that now I have you."

Lord, help me. He wished what she said was true.

Chapter Ten

ELEANOR NEEDED TO GET away from all these watchful eyes. Only then could she tell Ben what Mrs. Allan had told her when they'd been alone by the coffee beans. Besides warning her about Ben, Mrs. Allan had gossiped about the other stranger. And unlike the story about the Loch Ness monster, Eleanor suspected there was truth to the news.

She let Ben lead her on a winding path out of the village center, away from the nosy neighbors and over a few creeks. The longer they walked, the closer to the loch they moved, but not in the direct way Eleanor had anticipated. It was more that Ben led her alongside it, as if they approached the water cautiously rather than confront it.

Low clouds hung overhead, pressing down like a foreboding weight. Questions bubbled, but telling Ben about the other stranger was the priority. Yet, when she opened her mouth to tell him, another question—the real question that had been humming under her skin—slipped out entirely.

"Have you been in hiding from danger or staying away from home to avoid Mr. Brown's charges?"

His arm muscles flexed beneath her hand and she realized exactly what she said.

"Did I ask that right?" The words tumbled out and she stopped them in the middle of wherever they were, her heart pounding as the fear that had begun swirling since Mrs. Allan's conversation cinched a knot around her stomach. "Because, if you're in hiding, then I shouldn't have found you. I shouldn't have traveled here. I should have considered my actions before I let Cora shove me on a train. What was I thinking? I wasn't, that's what."

Ben turned to face her, dislodging her touch. She wrapped her arms around her middle and stepped back. She couldn't look at him. Couldn't face him. Here she'd arrived ready to save him and bring him home, but what if …

"Ben, what if I led someone dangerous to you?" Oh, she might be sick. She backed away from him as if she could retract her foolishness from causing him harm.

But Ben reached for her. "This is the side of a hill, El. You'll tumble."

"Oh!" She glanced over her shoulder. Sure enough, they were to the left of the water now and the slope led down to the lake—no, the loch—as if a mudslide had cleared a direct path through the trees. Perhaps it had. She stared at the water. "Be honest, Ben. Could you be in danger because of me?"

He stepped beside her, his arm brushing hers. She swayed toward his warmth, her body betraying her mind in favor of his comfort. She expected his rejection, yet his large hand touched her back and she stilled, waiting to see what he'd do. Perhaps he wondered the same because he didn't move either.

Birds tittered around them. A large shadow swooped along the blue water of the loch. Eleanor shuddered at the thought of a bird of prey hunting its unsuspecting food. Ben slid his hand to her opposite shoulder, tugging her into the shelter of his side. She rested her head in the crook of his shoulder. Sixteen years hadn't changed how safe she felt when he embraced her like this.

Except something had changed.

His thumb caressed her shoulder, bringing an awareness she hadn't noticed before. It caused her insides to swoop in a way she had never experienced. She raised her chin to discover Ben watching her, not the circling bird. Memory of the couple of kisses they shared as youths increased the speed at which her stomach flipped.

"Tell me about the man from the train." His chest rumbled with the lowness of his voice.

Reality crashed. If she brought danger to Ben, how could she entertain these romantic thoughts about him? It was the height of selfishness. She attempted to put distance between them, but Ben's hold tightened around her shoulders, drawing her even closer to his side.

"Do you think this stranger followed you all the way from Montana to Fort Augustus?" He sounded skeptical. Perhaps she'd let fear override logic?

Eleanor turned her attention to the loch or she'd never get the words out of her throat. "Mrs. Allan said the man was American and asking questions about you. She thinks he's a cop or detective searching for a fugitive, and warned me to stay away from you because you're, well ... I'm not sure the word she used exactly, but I take it that it means *bad news*."

Ben's chest bounced with a single laugh. "Have you seen this stranger before? On the train in America or here in Scotland? Or could he have been one of those men Hiram had to fend off while you were on the boat?"

She considered the question, forcing herself to return to a more rational line of thought. "I met a lot of strangers with American accents and broad shoulders on the trip here. Nothing about the way Mrs. Allan described him made him stand out. Perhaps if I saw him again, I could tell you."

"That's what I figured, and why I think we have to draw him out."

She risked looking at Ben again. "What if he is a detective searching for you?"

Ben's lips curved into a smile. "Probably is. And it's not the first time."

"Really?" Surprise had her leaning back and Ben adjusted his arm behind her to draw her close.

"Really." A twinkle sparked in his eye. Why wasn't he more worried about this than she was? "It's the reason I enlisted. Free ticket out of the country."

"To war."

"I'd already killed once." He shrugged as if taking a life wasn't serious. "After the Armistice, I returned to America and left the Navy. I considered coming home. I missed you."

Tears smarted. "I wish you would have." Selfish, selfish, selfish.

"I might have risked it, except I was recruited for another project and while I considered accepting, I felt someone following me." He rested his chin on her head. "My recruiter investigated and discovered Brown was still watching for me, was still wanting to press murder charges. If I returned home, I'd be tried for murder, and if that failed, Brown would simply have me exterminated. My recruiter not only believed my innocence, but found my skills too handy to risk letting Brown send an assassin after me. So he hustled me off to the Continent."

She knew Brown hadn't given up, but ... she eased away so she could see his face. "Who was this recruiter?"

Ben's eyes narrowed as if weighing her trustworthiness. "I'd like to wait to answer that."

Eleanor shivered, about to protest when another piece of the puzzle clicked into place. "It has something to do with Amalie and Max, doesn't it?" She couldn't guess at what exactly, but perhaps the reason Ben wasn't scared of the danger Brown could be was because he was facing it from another front entirely.

Ben dashed his thumb across her cheek, then quickly looked out over the loch, pulling her to his chest again. "My role has evolved over the years as I learned new languages and proved myself capable in dangerous situations. It became necessary to give me a hideaway, as you say, and that's how I came to live here at the edge of Loch Ness."

She sensed there was more to the story, but she wouldn't push. "Is there any chance you will ever return to Montana?" As soon as she asked the question, she wished to take it back. It bled with all the hope she'd packed into her luggage for the trip to Scotland.

Ben's arms flexed around her as he sighed. "I'd like to see my grandparents, sisters, and nieces again. But not until Brown stops hunting for me. My boss now agrees with my recruiter that Brown won't wait for legal channels. So you're right to worry that this stranger followed you from Montana to put an end to me."

Such emotional reality caused a deep chill to slither down her back, and a sense of hopelessness washed over her. She squeezed her eyes closed, dislodging a tear, two, three. This was all her fault. If she hadn't run into Georgie that day … If she had somehow been able to get free of him before Ben had to rescue her … But what could she have done differently? She hadn't even realized Georgie wanted a kiss, let alone … more.

A sob jerked up her throat, and Ben pressed her head to his chest.

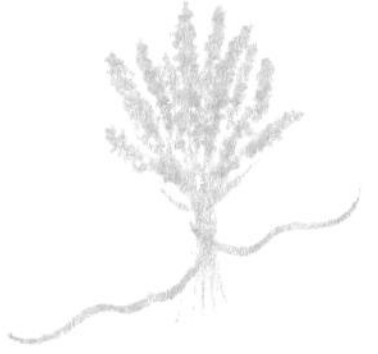

Chapter Eleven

"Hey, hey, no need for that now." Ben's heart cracked at hearing Eleanor cry. "If the American who followed you came hunting for me, I can manage that. I'm no stranger to thugs. Anyway, he'll stick out and I'll find him. Women like Mrs. Allan make for great lookouts. You don't have to worry, El."

Her cheek moved in a nod against his chest.

"It's better if he came for me than you." He closed his eyes. "I couldn't bear it if something happened to you."

"You're not mad that I led someone to you?" Her question came out muffled by Ben's coat and he almost laughed.

"No, of course not. I'm not worried for me." The thought of Eleanor getting hurt, though? Traveling across country was dangerous enough, but New York City as a beautiful woman? Traveling across an ocean, even with a chaperone? Men could be unscrupulous if they thought they could take advantage. *Oh, Lord, please no ....*

"El, Hiram hinted that I should ask you what you've had to endure the last sixteen years." His heart jumped into his throat. "I thought leaving would take the harm with me, that I could draw it away from you. Did I ... did I not do that? Did I leave you to fight the battle all on your own?"

"That's why you left?" She tugged away hard enough he let her go, but caught her hands so she couldn't go far. She searched his face and he couldn't hide his emotion from her.

"If I was sure justice would have been done, I would have let the courts run their course. But you know as well as I do that I would not have received the benefit of the doubt. And if I was acquitted, Brown would have taken matters into his own hands."

She pressed her lips together. He glanced over her shoulder, afraid to ask her again how she had fared the last sixteen years. His stomach churned. The way she'd been nervous about Mrs. Allan and her gossiping ways, the fact that she had never married, that she'd been able to drop everything and travel halfway around the world to find him. It all screamed at him that life had been anything but the rosy dream he'd wished for her.

"I'm—El, I'm sorry I wasn't there for you when you needed me."

Her beautiful blue eyes turned into a pair of watery lochs, cutting his heart to ribbons.

He tightened his grip on her hands, begging her to understand. "I thought saving other innocents would mollify my conscience for having taken a life, but I failed to realize that my leaving didn't protect the person I cared most about."

Eleanor's eyes widened. Did she not realize how much she meant to him? How much she didn't deserve a man like him loving her as much as he did?

"The thing is, El, I killed once, then in war I killed more." He stared at the cloudy sky, each face—each man he sent to God's judgment seat—flashing in his mind.

"I know how my grandfather is still feared as a beast, though he is a good man. I hate how relieved I am that my father is gone, considering the monster he was. Now, not only do I have a reputation as a murderer, I have killed. Whether justified because I was saving someone or because it happened in war … I have still taken lives. What kind of man does that make me?"

She said nothing, so he let go of her hands and stepped away.

"While it's true I left to avoid getting my neck in a noose and as much as I am grateful to see you again, I did leave to protect you. Or, at least, I thought it would protect you because I'm no good for you, El. I'm not the type of man who can love you the way you deserve. I haven't even protected you the way you needed. I'm sorry, El. I'm sorry you came all this way only for me to hurt you again."

"You love me?" Her voice wavered as if breathed into the wind.

What was love, really? The past sixteen years had changed his view of love. It wasn't this cloud-like emotion that put stars in his eyes. Love was hard. It was a choice to seek the best for the object of one's love. It was not selfish nor did it involve believing the worst of that someone.

The years had shown him just how many people did not love him. How could he love someone else? Perhaps he shouldn't have used that word so easily. Perhaps he should have said he *cared* for her, or felt *affection* for her. Yet he couldn't bring himself to make the correction. Because sixteen years ago, he'd been that starry-eyed lad in love with the girl who now stood behind him.

"Ben?" She placed a hand on his back. "Do you ... love me?"

His respiration increased as panic rose. He searched their surroundings as if danger hemmed them in. Animals played, a bird still circled overhead, no sign of anyone but them on this hillside. Yet danger felt close. Too close. Could it be the woman behind him that made him feel this way?

"Dearest Ben." She slipped her arm through his. "If we're being honest, I've always admired you. You were my protector, my friend. You were willing to follow an adventurous girl all over the Montana countryside, keeping her safe even when she put herself in harm's way."

A smile threatened. "Like the time you thought you'd help that baby bunny."

She swatted his stomach. "And I did."

"I had to kill the snake before it bit you."

"And before it ate the bunny, thank you very much."

Yes. That was Eleanor. He'd killed more than one snake for her, and he'd do it again.

"You have always made me feel safe. It's probably why I had a crush on you."

He glanced down just as she turned her chin away. Still, he caught the blush on her cheeks. He'd never been quite sure of her affection for him. Sure, she'd let him kiss her a couple times, but he hadn't been confident it meant as much to her as it had to him. She could have chosen any boy to court her, even that rat Georgie Brown.

Before he realized what she was about, she'd caught the lapels of his coat, pulled herself up to her toes, then gently placed her lips to his cheek. "I love you, too."

Then she dashed back the way they'd come, leaving him stunned on the side of the hill.

A caw overhead jerked him from his moment of dreamy insanity.

Instinct flared. He'd forgotten his vigilance and now the critters had gone quiet. The bird of prey overhead had been replaced by a triplet of vultures.

Something stalked nearby. Was it the Loch Ness monster or something of the human variety? He searched the surrounding area for what seemed amiss, then realized Eleanor had vanished from sight.

Eleanor!

Fear shot through him. This is why he was a failure at love. Death was his best companion.

He shook off the morbid thought and raced after her, praying he'd arrive before the next snake bit the only woman who would ever hold his heart.

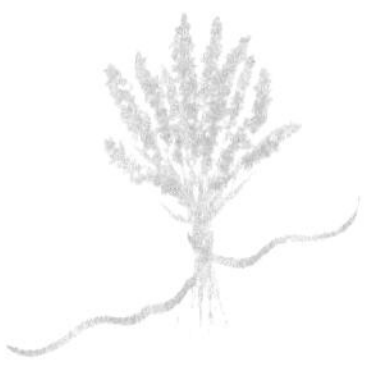

Chapter Twelve

WHAT WAS SHE DOING?

Eleanor's heart pounded and her conscience walloped her. No wonder all the gossips back in Blue Spruce thought her a loose woman.

She followed the path they'd taken from Bieldfell, though she wasn't sure she'd be able to find Agnes's home without Ben. In fact, she wasn't all that sure this was the right way back to town.

Eleanor stumbled to a stop, heart pounding for another reason. Where had the loch gone? She spun in a slow circle, realizing she was completely surrounded by trees now. Had they come this way from the grocers?

She opened her mouth to call out to Ben, but shame and humiliation kept her quiet. First, that she'd kiss him like that, second, that she admitted she loved him—something she would have to figure out for herself later—and third, that she'd gone off on her own only to get lost.

Lost in a foreign country.

She shivered. In Montana, if she got lost, the mountains served as a compass for the most part. Or the sun and stars allowed her to navigate relatively well. Here, she had no sense of direction. The sun was hidden behind darkening clouds. Damp cold she'd effectively ignored with Ben by her side slithered down her back.

As youths, Ben had always been rescuing her from situations like this, or joining her in the first place. Sixteen years later and she was just as foolish as a child. Worse, she let emotion, not curiosity, drive her.

Eleanor spun around again, listening for Ben. What if he couldn't find her? Or ... what if he never came looking for her? He never came back to Montana, and didn't think she should have tracked him down. Perhaps he was embarrassed by her declaration. She covered her face, her mortification complete.

What kind of woman traveled halfway around the world to find her childhood crush *sixteen* years after he left her? And when she finds him, she throws herself at him like one of the girls who worked in the Blue Spruce saloons.

Why had Cora encouraged this? Why had Silas seen her off on the train? Even Hiram supported this fool's errand. What did they see that she didn't? Surely those three individuals—people she looked up to for their relationship with God and the respectful way they treated her—would have warned her of an unwise path.

Rustling nearby caused her heart to skip. Had Ben found her? That thought filled her with both elation and trepidation. What would she say when she saw him again?

A rabbit scampered past in a blur of white fur and big ears.

Eleanor sank to the ground. Though the cold seeped into her backside, her limbs couldn't hold her up. The chill thawed her emotions, allowing the survival skills she knew from living in Montana to rise. She'd allow herself two minutes more to wallow and sputter, then she'd straighten up and … did she find Ben or try to find Agnes's home? Perhaps she'd start by calling out to Ben.

She rested her head in her hands, elbows on her knees. Indecision froze her. Now that she'd found Ben, and he could not return to Montana, did she and Hiram return home? If the American stranger was after Ben, that might be the best option. They might draw him away or Ben could disappear again until the man gave up. But Ben's grandparents would be devastated.

In all honesty, so would she. Until this moment, she hadn't realized just how much hope she'd placed on finding Ben. Yet nothing about this reunion was anything like she dreamed it would be. She rubbed her abdomen. Pie in the sky, like that song said.

Eleanor pushed to her feet. Time to stop living like the sixteen-year-old who watched her world crumble in a single afternoon. She was twice that age now. It was time to set aside childish things, which started by getting herself out of the mess she'd caused.

If only she could figure out which way was home.

Wisdom told her not to let pride or shame dictate, so she gathered her breath and called Ben's name. Closing her eyes, she listened for his answer.

"Call again, I'll find you!" His words were faint, but they did something to her insides she had no business feeling.

Still, she grinned and called his name again.

Rustling to her left had her smile widening and relief washing over her. She braced for Ben's teasing, ready to admit she shouldn't have run off and gotten herself lost. Though, if she were back home, she wouldn't have gotten lost. She had a good sense of direction, except that this place was all new.

Branches swayed and a man emerged.

A man. Not Ben.

She backed up, ready to call out to Ben again, to tell him to stay away. This had to be the American stranger, right?

Except he held up his hand, palm toward her. "Miss Finch? My name is Jim Taylor. I'm not here to harm you."

Ben crashed through the trees. "Next time …" his words trailed off as he took in the scene.

In one smooth move, Mr. Taylor had put himself between Eleanor and Ben, his gun pointed at Ben's chest. Ben answered, not with surrender, but with his pistol aimed at Mr. Taylor.

Eleanor stepped to the side and Mr. Taylor waved her back. "I won't let him hurt you, Miss Finch. Stay behind me."

"I'm not hurting her." Ben growled. "Who are you?"

"Name's Jim Taylor." The tall, wide-shouldered man braced his gun with both hands. "I'm here to bring you back to Blue Spruce to face the justice you deserve."

"He's not guilty." Eleanor shifted around the man, but wasn't crazy enough to step between the two. "Would you two lower your pistols, please. I'd like to not get shot."

The men didn't budge.

Eleanor rolled her eyes. "Mr. Taylor, I'm the witness to Ben's supposed crime. If I say he's not guilty, why don't you believe me?"

He dashed her a look of compassion, and she realized she had seen him before. He'd never approached her, but they'd been on the same boat across the Atlantic. "You don't have to defend him, Miss Finch. I won't let him coerce you into lying for him. You're safe now."

Eleanor's jaw dropped. Is that what people thought?

Ben scoffed. "Look, Taylor—or whatever your name is—you'll have to shoot me before I go anywhere with you.

And I promise you, I have no problem putting a bullet in you if you go anywhere near that trigger."

"Ben!" Eleanor glared at him. "Do you want him to shoot you?"

The corner of his mouth tipped up. "Yeah. Then I have reasonable cause to defend myself."

Eleanor groaned, but Taylor cracked a smile. She stared at him, surprised at the respect that shown in his eyes.

"I have an assignment, but I'm willing to call a truce." Taylor lifted his left hand in surrender, though he kept his gun aimed at Ben. "What do you say? We talk this out like men instead of fight it out like gunslingers?"

Eleanor clasped her hands together and held her breath. Would Ben take this olive branch?

Ben raised his left hand to match Mr. Taylor's stance. "On the count of three, then."

Mr. Taylor nodded. Ben counted off by lowering one finger at a time. When only his forefinger and thumb were left, both men lowered their weapons. Eleanor deflated, resting her back against a tree to keep her knees from giving out.

"Jim Taylor." The man holstered his weapon. "I'm a bounty hunter for hire and Mr. Brown had reason to believe Miss Finch had located you. I've been watching her for several weeks, though I admit to being surprised with how quickly she managed to get her travel plans lined up without any warning."

"I'm right here," she muttered, but wouldn't admit to the fact she had nothing to do with those plans. That had been the Wards' doing.

"I appreciate your honesty." Ben holstered his weapon. "To tell you the truth, I have no intention of leaving with you. If you'd like to hear my side of the story, then you're welcome to help me escort Miss Finch to her chaperones."

Eleanor straightened. "Are you sure—"

"I'm a fair man, Ford." Taylor rested his hands on his belt. "I'm not a gun for hire. I believe in bringing the guilty to the courts and protecting the innocent."

Ben grinned. "Then we'll get along just fine."

Eleanor folded her arms. "Have you ever seen two mountain goats in the spring?"

The men looked at her in surprise, as if they'd both forgotten she was there. Figured.

Eleanor shook her head and marched off, not caring if she had the right direction or not. Whatever emotion had gotten her lost in the first place was long gone. "If you haven't, gentlemen, then take a look in the mirror. I'm going ..."

Home.

Chapter Thirteen

NIGHT HAD LONG-AGO FALLEN before the grown-ups could talk without little ears listening in. Namely Amalie. Ben filled his cup with tea from the pot Agnes had made. The little girl had stayed up way past her bedtime, manufacturing ways to return to the kitchen, and forcing them to wait until they were sure she was sound asleep before settling around the table.

Of course, Max had woken, but Hiram surprised them all by offering to feed him so Agnes could join the discussion. Ben would have thought Hiram would have insisted on staying for Eleanor's sake, but the look the older man sent Agnes suggested he knew more about her than most.

Ben cast a glance at his Scottish friend. She hid a lot of secrets, knew a lot of people all over the world. Ben only knew that she kept his secrets; he didn't know any of hers. So what would she have shared with Hiram, and why?

A mystery for another evening. Right now, he needed to decide how to handle Jim Taylor. The man was about his age, if a little older, though the grizzled spots of gray hair and tanned, weathered skin could lie. As Ben knew well. Taylor could handle a gun, that was obvious, but what intrigued Ben the most was Taylor's sense of justice.

Why would Brown hire someone who could change his mind when presented with the truth?

Ben turned from the stove, mug in hand. Taylor had taken the chair beside Eleanor and Ben had his answer. Brown had used Taylor's affection for Eleanor. Ben clenched his jaw, knowing his beard would hide the motion. Intimidation wouldn't work here, it would only drive Taylor closer to Eleanor.

But would that be for the best?

"You're rather quiet." Agnes poured herself a cuppa. "Did you offer him tea?"

Ben snorted. "He looked offended that I suggested it."

"Like Hiram." Agnes sipped. "I'll bring him around, I suspect. But thank you for bringing the coffee."

Ben had almost forgotten the sack on the side of the hill, but after the confrontation with Taylor, Eleanor had stomped off back toward where she'd first left him. He still hadn't figured out why she kept storming away from him. She never used to do that. Or had she, and he'd blocked it from his mind? It'd been a long time.

"What do you think of him?" Agnes pointed her chin toward Taylor, who sat too close to Eleanor.

"He has a sense of justice, so maybe he'll listen." Ben grunted. "I'd hate to add to my body count where Eleanor is concerned."

Agnes laughed, drawing Eleanor and Taylor's attention. Enough with delaying the inevitable. Ben purposefully took the chair across from Eleanor and Taylor, knowing it would feel more like an interrogation than a conversation. Agnes sat at the end of the table, the mediator, though Ben trusted her to have his back.

Eleanor met his gaze, worry in her eyes. He should have kicked Taylor out of his chair. Instead, he eased his foot forward, hoping to connect with Eleanor's shoe. The gentle smile that softened her nervousness told him he succeeded. It would have to be enough for now.

Taylor folded his hands and rested them on the table. "I would like to hear Eleanor's side of the story, but I fear she will be intimidated with you here. Is there a chance you would step out for a few minutes?"

"No." Ben stared him down. "I'll share my side of the story. If Eleanor wishes to add anything, she's welcome to do so, but I will not have her forced to relive that day."

Eleanor covered her mouth and a tear slipped down her cheek.

Ben fisted his hands to keep from reaching for her. He'd protect her, even if it made proving his innocence more difficult. It's one of the reasons why he'd left. In hindsight, perhaps he should have taken her with him. But she'd have never left her mother, and he'd had no means of providing for them back then.

"Start from the beginning, then." Taylor leaned back, arms crossed.

Ben took one look at the ceiling, sending up a prayer he hoped God would hear for Eleanor's sake, then let his mind return to that awful April day. "My grandmother had sent me to town for a list of things from the grocer's. Before I picked up the items, I circled around to the back of the laundry where Eleanor and her mother worked, so I hoped I could distract Eleanor for a few minutes."

"You were eighteen at the time?" Taylor asked.

Ben nodded. "El and I have been friends since I first learned my mother's friend would have a baby. I admit to being disappointed it wasn't a boy, but from early on, she kept up with me." He couldn't help smiling at the memory of their childhood antics. He'd dare her to do things he thought a girl couldn't do, then she'd do them better than he could. Instead of it being a blow to his boyhood, he found a best friend. Someone he could escape with when his father's fists started flying.

Eleanor reached across the table. "My mother missed yours until the day Mama died."

Ben clenched his jaw against the emotion, then pried it loose to keep talking. "You should know, Taylor, that my father killed my mother, then died in prison. Is it any wonder people assume I'm the same type of man?"

Taylor didn't react, which told Ben the man already knew. He'd probably met his grandfather, too, and heard the scandalmongers expound how the man was a beast to be feared. Never mind that he was the kindest man Ben had ever met and was nothing like his monster of a father.

So which man was Ben truly like? His mother's father, or his own?

"When I reached the alley behind the laundry, Eleanor was already outside." Ben couldn't look at her as he told this part. He wished she would excuse herself so she didn't need to be reminded of it. "She wasn't alone and it took only a glance to understand Georgie Brown—"

Eleanor's quiet sob sliced into him. He slammed his fists on the table, propelling himself to his feet. Taylor's right hand drifted toward his weapon, his left toward Eleanor's arm. He touched her and she flinched, igniting Ben's rage.

He leaned his palms on the table, leaning close to Taylor, daring him to pull the gun on him again. "I don't regret stepping in to save her. If Brown hadn't pulled a knife on me, he might still be alive, but I wasn't about to let him kill me so he could go back to torturing my friend."

Taylor showed no reaction, no hint whether he believed Ben or not.

Ben shoved away from the table. "I need some air."

His hand was on the doorknob when Eleanor stopped him. "He didn't pull the knife on you, Ben. He'd already used it on me."

Chapter Fourteen

E LEANOR TREMBLED, BUT KNEW she had to share the part of the story that only the doctor—and Georgie—knew. "You saved my life, Ben, even more than you understand."

Ben turned from the door, confusion softening the anger that had erupted from him. He searched her face, and she fought not to hide, though she didn't know what he looked to find.

Hiram appeared without Max, so he must have gotten the child to sleep. The older man met Eleanor's gaze with one of question—was she alright? She wasn't, but she had to take this step. Hiram nodded and took Ben's seat, shifting it toward Agnes who sat to Eleanor's left.

The older woman had stayed quiet and Eleanor couldn't discern what she thought of all of this. Did she know Ben's story already? It hadn't seemed to surprise her, so she probably did. In fact, now that Eleanor thought about it, the older lady appeared as protective of Ben as Hiram was of Eleanor. Eleanor ducked her head, giving in to the need to hide herself. If Agnes knew her secret, would she protect Ben from her? Throw her out? Send her back to America?

Then there was Jim Taylor. She knew he worried Ben coerced her to lie for him. If anything, the opposite was true. Her secret had been twisted and used against her when it could have been used to free Ben of guilt. Though wasn't the law innocence until guilt was proven? That wasn't the case for Ben. For her neither. The law of public opinion had woven their tale, declared their guilt, and sentenced them accordingly. Ben had escaped before George Brown could execute the penalty he thought Ben deserved. Eleanor ... had not.

She squeezed her eyes shut, wishing she could vanish from this room. Would anything have changed if Ben hadn't run from his presumed guilt? If he'd stayed, she might have told him. He'd have realized she kept a secret—back then, he'd recognized her moods as if they were his own. However, she wouldn't have wanted anyone else to know. It would have taken Ben a herculean effort to pry it out of her. But he would have done it, she had no doubt. Of course, her secret would have likely come out in the court proceedings if Ben had been tried. More proof he'd been justified in protecting her. That his quick actions had saved her life. That the knife Georgie wielded had already been unsheathed before their wrestling had landed it in Georgie's chest.

Eleanor shuddered. She hated reliving those moments, though she must face them now. Ben deserved that and more. If only it didn't transport her to that day sixteen years ago. The icy cold that had crept through her body. The helplessness as Ben fought for his life, and hers. The way death had snapped its fingers and ended the lives of three young people that day. She needed courage now.

What had their new president said back in March, at his inaugural address? She'd joined Mrs. Cox, her son and daughter-in-law, the Wards, and the others staying at Mrs. Cox's boarding house as they all gathered around the radio to listen to Mr. Roosevelt's first speech as president. It had been rousing, confidence-building, a message of hope and unity. But a sentence had jumped out at her, though she didn't know why at the time. Perhaps God had pointed it out for this moment.

This is no unsolvable problem if we face it wisely and courageously.

She could do this. She could offer Ben the vindication he deserved for rescuing her all those years ago. They may go their separate ways after this, but now, here, she could offer him this gift.

A blanket was draped over her shoulders. She raised her gaze to see Ben standing over her, a look in his eyes she had never seen before. It was soft, caring, gentle. So unlike the dark-haired, tattooed mountain man he portrayed. Bravery fought against fear. It was time.

Taylor shifted his chair to keep Ben in his sights, Eleanor was sure. She turned her chair, too, though it put Agnes and Hiram at her back. Better to forget about them right now or her courage may fail. Ben squatted at her knee and she gripped his hands, drawing from his strength. Though there were other people in the room, others listening, she would focus on telling him this part of the story.

"I'd just finished ironing a pile of shirts for Mama, and gone outside to get a break from the steam of the laundry while the irons reheated." Eleanor concentrated on Ben's rough hands. An inked vine trailed out from under his sleeve and she traced the leaf with her thumb. "I didn't see Georgie before he pinned me to the wall."

"You don't have to share the details, Miss Finch." Taylor had leaned forward, elbows on his knees, pain deepening the brackets around his frown. It meant much that he'd give this way out of revealing her deepest pain. "I came here to see justice, not cause you harm."

His kindness bolstered her and she continued on. "Ben showed up before Georgie could do what I suspect he wanted. But that angered Georgie and ..." She glanced up at the ceiling as if that could keep her tears at bay.

"What did I miss?" Ben whispered, and she knew he was remembering the scene, searching it like a detective analyzing a crime.

She swallowed and met his dark eyes. "He stabbed me just before you yanked him away."

"What?" Ben sounded as if he'd been punched in the stomach. Pain and anger flashed across his features. As a youth, he'd been strong, a protector, a defender. Now, dark, mysterious, and muscle-bound, he radiated power like a gladiator.

It should scare her, perhaps, but instead she felt empowered. She pressed her palm against the lowest part of her abdomen and continued, infusing gratefulness to soften the blow she'd dealt. "Ben, the doctor said it was a shallow, straight stab because you pulled Georgie off of me so quickly. I lived though I'd been stabbed in the gut. Don't you see? It could have been much, much worse."

Even with his beard, Eleanor could see how tightly Ben clenched his jaw.

She tried again to get through to him, squeezing the rough hands she still held. "Your quick actions saved me, Ben. The doctor was able to patch me up." She left off the worst of it. For now, it seemed wisest. Or perhaps simply cowardly.

Ben's throat bobbed beneath his beard. "Why ... El, why didn't you tell me?"

"I like to think I would have." If he'd stayed. But she wouldn't heap that guilt on him. "But between Mr. Brown and the gossips, the story went in a different direction, and I was so humiliated by what people said of me, I begged the doctor to keep it quiet. I didn't even tell my mother all of it."

"All of it?" Ben pressed. Of course, he caught her slip. This was the part she'd kept secret from everyone. The part not even Mama or the sheriff knew about.

Ben's face turned into a watery blur as the tears spilled down her cheeks. There went her courage. She could talk about her injury, attempt to convince Ben of how he saved her, but ... this? It was her shame, made worse by the rumors the gossips had spread.

Another hand pressed her shoulder. "I think that's enough for today, gentlemen." Agnes. Could she sense that Eleanor needed the protection of another woman right now? It caused another wave of emotion to crash over her, loosening her grip on the anguish inside.

"No." Ben's voice was strangled and she wasn't sure which of them held the other's hand tighter. "My imagination is running wild. Please tell me. Everyone else can leave, but El, please. I need to know."

His pleading only made her cry harder. If she told him, would he reject her? He thought her a woman worth protecting, but in the back of her mind she felt ... less. Though the gossips claimed it was because she'd been ruined by a man, perhaps they were right that no other man would ever want her.

"Would you like him to know?" Agnes slid her arm over Eleanor's shoulders, her voice gentle yet firm. Like she knew Eleanor's secret without saying a word and did not judge her for it.

Eleanor squeezed her swollen eyes closed and nodded. Not that she could tell Ben right now, but Agnes's comfort told her that at least one person would stand by her side. This secret. It had eaten at her, kept her chained for sixteen years. Could she finally release it? Tell the one person whose reaction she feared the most?

"I'm going to take a guess." Agnes spoke just loudly enough to be heard over the tears Eleanor couldn't stop. Had Hiram and Taylor left or were they about to witness her shame, too? "Based on what you've said—and stop me if you wish this to stay quiet—you cannot have children now, can you?"

Hearing the words spoken out loud for the first time since the doctor had compassionately delivered the news cracked Eleanor's heart. Ben's hand disappeared—whether he said words or not, she didn't hear him—and it ripped her soul in two. She felt, more than heard, people leaving the room, or perhaps the cabin based on the damp breeze that caressed her tear-streaked face. They despised her and left her as she'd always be. Alone.

Then arms lifted her. Strong, muscular arms that carried the scent of grass and sheep and wild things. With gentle motion, as if she were a lamb, Ben set her on his lap. She curled into him as he wrapped her in a tight embrace. His beard brushed her temple, and a splash landed on her flushed cheek. His chest heaved as his tears mingled with her own.

And he rocked them until she fell asleep.

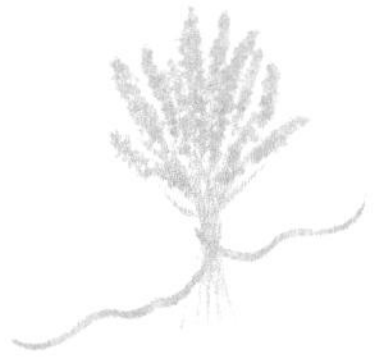

Chapter Fifteen

T HOUGH HIS MOOD REMAINED dark, Ben revelled in the rare bit of sunshine that warmed the air the following morning, as well as the walk that eased his sore muscles. Sitting in a hard chair all night proved he wasn't as young anymore, but he wouldn't have traded the time spent holding Eleanor for all the down-filled mattresses in the world.

He had some personal wrestling to do about the news she revealed last night. It would start with a conversation with Jim Taylor, after he stopped by the telegraph office to see whether Otto had made it safely into England. If no news arrived, he'd inform Agnes that inquiries would need to be made. For Max's sake, they needed to know whether his guardian was still alive.

For that matter, he needed to make a decision on what to do about Amalie. Her parents had left her in his care, which made little sense. A man like him couldn't be her father. He had no wife, he disappeared on secret missions with no notice, and had but a shepherd's hut that he called home. Though the beautiful blonde-haired woman he'd held in his arms all night could change all of that.

He yanked open the door to the telegraph office harder than necessary. Though in his eighteen-year-old mind, he thought himself noble for leaving Blue Spruce, maturity suggested he'd been selfish. He thought he'd be saving Eleanor by removing his bloodied hands from her life. Now he realized he'd left her to face it all alone.

"Got a message for you." The telegraph operator handed it over and scurried away. Trustworthy, but skittish, especially when Ben didn't soften his visage.

He blew out a breath and tore open the envelope. He couldn't manage everyone else today, so he'd focus on the most important. Eleanor. And the children. A smile tugged at his mouth. Otto had made it across the Channel and would arrive shortly. Today, even, depending on how quickly this telegraph traveled through the maze of security Ben had set up. Max would see his new father again.

He left the office, headed to the boardinghouse to find Taylor.

It warmed Ben's heart to see family reunited. Though he never wished to see his late father again, he longed for a conversation with his grandfather. The one regret he had about never returning home was not knowing whether he had his grandfather's forgiveness. If Caleb Orson could grant mercy, perhaps Ben would finally believe that God could grant mercy, too.

Not that Grandfather was god-like. He was scary, and stern, and a beast of a man who expected others to live with integrity. Ben wanted to live up to his grandfather's expectations, but being his father's son, he was never sure it was possible.

Which was why he couldn't be Amalie's father. Or have a relationship with Eleanor. If he closed his eyes, he could still feel her sleeping against his chest. As a youth, he'd been enamored with her, loved her as only a boy could his best friend. Now, those were but childish emotions. The woman Eleanor had become ... brave, strong, courageous, daring ... Her spirit called to him like a lantern in a blizzard, lighting the way home.

"Figured you'd come around this morning." Taylor met him outside the boardinghouse. "Let's walk up by the Abbey."

Ben fell into step with the man. Slightly older than Ben and a couple inches shorter, Jim Taylor wore his years well. He had a wizened air about him, similar to Hiram. Except, where Hiram was mischievous, Taylor exuded silent calculation. Ben could see the wheels of the man's mind turning even now.

"How's your girl this morning?" Taylor asked as they crossed the road. *Your girl.*

Fortunately, the bells of the Abbey chimed ten o'clock and Ben waited until the sound faded before he answered. "Agnes treated her like a mother hen does her chick."

"Didn't take you for a poet, Ford."

"Didn't expect you to pry into my relationship with Eleanor."

Taylor laughed. "Does she know how much you love her?"

"Who says I do?" This wasn't the conversation Ben wanted to have with the man.

"Liar." Taylor grunted. "Only a man in love acts like you did last night. You would have throttled me for even bringing up the event I needed to understand, then you about climbed out of your skin as she relived that … event."

Ben clenched his jaw and they turned past the bell tower toward the loch. "Have you heard the rumors about the monster?"

"Who hasn't?" Taylor stared out over the water. "Think he's real?"

Ben crossed his arms. "I think people vilify what they don't understand. What they think is different, alien. Outside of what they consider *normal*."

"Are we talking about the Loch Ness monster or you, Ben?" Taylor turned and rested his hind end on the stone wall that surrounded the Abbey grounds. "Or even Eleanor?"

Ben scuffed his boot on the dirt. "Perhaps I mean all of us. Children like Amalie and Max, too."

"What's going to happen to those two?"

"Max's adopted father is on his way to take him to safety." Ben watched a black dog—probably a Scottish

Terrier—sniff at the Abbey's foundation, then dart back to a child and his parents. "They'll have a chance at a happy family, the boy with a father who will love him no matter his disability."

"I haven't met someone like him before. Aren't there institutions for people with, what is it called, Mongolism?"

"He doesn't belong in an institution." The words erupted from Ben like a volcano. "Have you seen that child? He's happy and sweet and deserves to be loved, not locked away like some ... some ... monster. If anyone is a monster, it's someone who disowns their own child because he's different."

"Sorry." Taylor paced away, then back. "Look, this is new for me, okay? I track down criminals, murderers, and send them to the courts to be tried. I don't make decisions on innocence and guilt. I don't decide who is a monster or who is not. I'm a deliveryman."

Ben stepped into his path. "Are you going to deliver me to my accuser?"

"That was my plan until last night." Taylor turned his back, took three steps, then stopped. "I can't do it, Ford. I was up all night after hearing Eleanor's story. That woman shouldn't have to prove her innocence to her neighbors."

Taylor's honesty had Ben responding in kind. "If I'd stayed, she wouldn't have had to face that alone for sixteen years."

"You know Brown won't stop until you're dead." Taylor squared off. "I know now why he chose me to follow Eleanor. He preyed on my sense of nobleness and knew I'd defend Eleanor against you. He hoped it'd be enough for me to bring you in."

The hairs on Ben's neck rose. "Did you sense someone following you?"

Taylor shook his head. "But I thought about it all night, and I'm confident Brown has a backup plan. He had to know the risk. Sending a man like me could end with the opposite of his wishes. Which is exactly what happened."

"He's a money man. He knows risk and reward." Ben planted his hands on his hips. "Do you think he sent another bounty man, or an assassin?"

"Don't know. But the last three years have hit him hard in the wallet. You've heard about the depression back home? I'm not entirely sure how Brown held onto his bank."

"Is anyone investigating that angle?" Ben mentally worked through scenarios. "Perhaps the financial pressure could get him to back off."

"Or make him more desperate." Taylor cocked his head. "What does he have to gain by your death? Other than revenge?"

"That's motive enough, in my book." Ben had killed for Eleanor, had killed for Amalie, for his brothers-in-arms, and others.

"Yeah, but you defend. Brown takes."

"That doesn't help us right now." His mind hurt from the emotional night and lack of sleep. "He's going to keep sending people until I'm dead. And Eleanor is going to get caught in the middle."

Taylor glanced at him out of the corner of his eye. "Then maybe we kill you."

He couldn't believe he wanted to admit the idea had merit.

"Hear me out." Taylor raised his hand as if he expected Ben to balk. "If Brown thinks you're dead, he won't chase you. It's why you disappeared in the first place. Now we know Brown has raised the stakes. We fake your death and you're free."

If it were only about him, he wouldn't hesitate. "What about Eleanor?"

Taylor raised his brows. "She'll return home with news of your death and be safe again. Or are you going to admit I was right about your feelings for her?"

"We can't fake her death, too." And what about Amalie? And his grandparents would mourn him. He couldn't do that to them. "No. It's a good idea, I admit, but I can't."

"You can't keep fending off every gunman Brown sends at you. He knows how to get to you now. You can no longer hide, because if you do, you might as well fake your death. It's the same thing."

Ben fisted his hands.

"I'd prefer it if you didn't slug the messenger."

A laugh shot out, surprising him.

Taylor grinned. "I think this is a conversation that requires your lady's input."

"She's not—"

"If you finish that sentence, I *will* slug you."

Ben dropped his chin. "I hate you, Taylor."

"Then the feeling is mutual." Taylor slapped Ben's shoulder. "Let's find a way to get you out of this mess once and for all so you can live that sappy happily ever after you're insisting doesn't exist for the likes of you."

The only happily ever after he could envision included Eleanor, and he could never ask her to join him in the mission he felt God had called him to carry out. Too many children's lives were at stake to indulge in his own happiness. Could he convince Eleanor—and his own heart—it had to be this way?

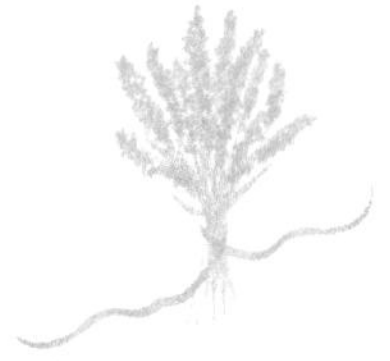

Chapter Sixteen

ELEANOR SAT IN AGNES'S rocking chair, sipping the cup of tea she'd pressed into her hands. It warmed Eleanor from the inside—both the tea and Agnes's kindness—and the steam eased the gritty soreness around her eyes.

The last time she'd cried so hard was the day Mama died. Then, she had cried in the solace of her rooms. Here, everyone had seen her tears, heard her shame, and yet she hadn't been rejected like she'd feared. Instead, Agnes mothered her as she bustled about the house. Hiram quietly brandished his rapier wit as Max babbled happily in his arms. And Amalie ...

"What's this?" Eleanor asked as the little girl approached with her hands behind her back.

Blond braids framed her pale face. Sorrow lingered in her blue eyes, but she smiled and shoved a bouquet of wildflowers at Eleanor. "For you."

Eleanor blinked back fresh tears. "For me? Thank you, Amalie." She set down her mug to take the stems, then pressed the yellow and blue blossoms to her nose.

Amalie twisted, her cotton dress swirling about her knees. "Frauline Agnes said I ..." She raised her eyes to the ceiling.

Eleanor laid the flowers beside her mug on the side table. "I'll help you find the word. What did Agnes say?" Agnes watched from the kitchen area with a look of approval.

A faint blush rose on Amalie's cheeks. "I listened last night. After Max fell asleep."

Oh. "You heard what I told the grown-ups." Eleanor's stomach churned.

Amalie nodded. "Frauline said I ask for ... for ..." Her nose scrunched in confusion.

"Forgiveness?" Eleanor took a guess.

Amalie nodded. "Like saying sorry. But I am not sorry."

"You aren't?" Curious, Eleanor rested her elbows on her knees so she could be closer to Amalie's level and block out the audience from the kitchen. "Why not?"

"You have no *kinder*. I have no papa or—" Amalie's sniffed, a tear slipping down her cheek.

"Amalie, dear one." Eleanor opened her arms, their shared grief breaking her heart. "I lost my mama and papa, too."

"You did?" She climbed onto Eleanor's lap. "They were killed? Ben saved you?"

Eleanor ran her hand over Amalie's head. "I never knew my papa. He died when I was a baby. My mama grew ill, then she went to heaven."

"Ben?" A light slowly awakened in Amalie's eyes. Not a sparkle of mischievousness, more like hope.

Footsteps and voices filtered in from outside. Eleanor tensed as Hiram handed Max to Agnes, took the rifle from above the cupboards, and peeked out the door. The relaxing of Hiram's shoulders told Eleanor it was likely Ben. Her stomach fluttered with nervous anticipation. He'd disappeared as soon as she woke up this morning.

Woke up in his arms. He'd held her all night in that hard chair.

The fluttering increased, and she returned her focus to the little girl on her lap. "Yes, Ben saved me. Did you hear that part of the story last night?"

Amalie nodded, then rested her head against Eleanor's shoulder. "He saved me like that."

Meaning he'd killed to save her? Eleanor wrapped her arms around the little girl, a fierce protectiveness shooting through her limbs. Had Ben felt this same protectiveness toward Eleanor last night, or had he held her with such tenderness because he felt something far different, something more?

"Eleanor?" Amalie whispered as Hiram opened the door wider and Ben and Jim Taylor entered the small cottage.

"Hmm?" Eleanor couldn't take her eyes from Ben as his gaze quickly swept the house, only to stop when it met hers.

"You have no kinder, I have no mama."

Eleanor tore her attention from the man who called to her heart. This little girl needed her. "This is true, dear one."

Amalie crooked her neck to look up at Eleanor. "Will you be my mama?"

Eleanor froze. Her heart stopped. The entire house ceased to breathe. Everyone of them stared at the little girl on her lap. Ben moved first, thank God, because Eleanor couldn't think. He knelt before them despite the hard floor, one large hand on Amalie's shoulder, his other resting on Eleanor's knee.

Amalie lifted her head from Eleanor's shoulder. "Ben, you can be my papa."

Eleanor's heart cracked. The idea that the three of them could be a family? It had never occurred to her, never had such a concept entered her dreams. Yet it sprouted hope within the barrenness of her soul. Beautiful, impractical hope.

"I am honored, Amalie." Ben smiled tenderly. "Your papa entrusted me with your care. I could never replace him, but I promise you I will always look out for you. And I know Eleanor will as well."

Amalie's little body folded in on itself. "But not as my mama and papa."

Ben lifted her chin. "A mama and papa are married, Amalie. That is something Eleanor and I would have to talk about between ourselves."

Eleanor's heart skipped. What would it be like to be married to Ben? To always have his care and protection, to love him and be loved in return?

"Get married soon!" Amalie wiggled off Eleanor's lap and skipped across the room. "Frauline Agnes, I am hungry."

The grown-ups in the room chuckled. Hiram and Mr. Taylor both sent winks, and Agnes bore a self-satisfied grin. For some reason, their approval washed away the lingering sense of shame. Though, based on the pinkening along Ben's cheekbones, it did embarrass him. Yet, he hadn't moved his hand from her knee or risen from the hard ground.

Ben cleared his throat. "I guess we should probably talk, huh?" No smile, no wink, he didn't even meet her eye. A niggle of unease dampened the good feelings inside. She nodded, unsure how to answer him.

Then she realized he'd never agreed with Amalie's idea. He affirmed that they would care for her, but not together. In fact, he seemed to go out of his way to make sure Amalie understood their care for her would be separate. After the way he held her last night, had morning brought a different understanding? Did he realize now that she wasn't worthy to be a wife?

A knock at the door startled everyone. Agnes gathered the children as the men readied to defend them. Eleanor couldn't convince herself to stand as she watched the muscles in Ben's back contract under his shirt as he opened the front door. Prepared. Lethal.

A tall, blond-haired man entered and immediately embraced Ben. "*Got sei dank.*"

"Otto." Ben slapped his back. "Thank God."

"Onkle Otto!" Amalie squealed and Otto caught her in a hug as she raced across the kitchen.

"You have grown, Amalie." Otto grinned, but even from this distance, Eleanor could see the deep lines etched into his wan face. "Where's Max?"

Hiram brought the little one forward, and from behind him, someone let out a cry. The blonde-haired woman rushed forward and pulled the child into her arms, tears falling on the little one's fuzzy hair. The other woman who had followed Otto inside wrapped her arm around the first woman's shoulder.

Otto closed the front door, his German accent thick but understandable as he explained. "This is Max's mother, Frieda, and her sister, Heda. Frieda did not agree to give up her baby, so I could not leave her behind."

Eleanor's legs refused to allow her to stand. Someone had taken this baby from his mother? Because he looked a little different than other babies? What kind of atrocity was that?

Ben folded his arms. "Will her husband let her go?"

"He's a—" Otto spat on the ground— "brownshirt. He will be too busy terrorizing other innocent people while working for the *Sturmabteilung*."

Frieda sniffed, still holding her baby tightly. "He wished to join the *Schutzstaffel*, so he could not have a child like Max."

"Your husband is SS?" Ben shoved his hands through his hair, paced to the window, and back. "They need to disappear, Otto."

"I know." Otto crossed his arms. "I delayed to bring Heda across. I will see them into hiding. Then I go back."

"You can't." Ben slashed his hand through the air. "If you get caught, you could ruin our whole operation."

Eleanor rose then, understanding bringing everything into sharp focus. Ben's hiding, his sometimes-lethal rescues, his hesitation at Amalie's idea of family. He wasn't just on the run from being accused of murder. He had a secret life, an undercover life. She glanced at Agnes. The woman knew, too, and that's how she'd found Ben's family. Found Eleanor. Contacts that somehow allowed Cora to find them.

Frieda gasped as she caught sight of Eleanor. "Are you *Deutsch*?"

"No," Ben answered for Eleanor. "She's visiting from America. Otto, I think you, Hiram, and Jim Taylor, here, should escort the women back to Montana. Frieda and Heda will find a home in Blue Spruce. Amalie can stay with you, Eleanor. And I—"

"She must help you." Frieda waved a shaking finger at Eleanor, an odd intensity lighting her blue eyes. "She must go to *Deutschland*."

Already reeling from Ben's words, Eleanor took a step back, her heart rate accelerating. "Go where?"

"She looks *Deutsch*?" Frieda's voice rose. "She can be an SS officer's *Freundin*. Infiltrate, get inside information, save other children like Max."

Eleanor's head was shaking before she even realized she made the motion. Her body trembled. "I ... I can't." Panic swirled inside. She couldn't face another man like Georgie Brown. A man who would give away his own child because he was different. No. Eleanor couldn't have anything to do with a man like that.

"You have to." Frieda shrieked, and Max began to cry. "You look like what my husband thinks is perfection. You have to help. Or you just another selfish woman who only cares about herself?"

"Frieda," Ben spoke, but Eleanor couldn't hear him.

The air around Eleanor disappeared as if she'd climbed to the top of one of the peaks west of Blue Spruce. Her vision narrowed to a long tunnel. Her ears buzzed like thousands of bees.

Selfish woman.

How many times had the gossips in Blue Spruce called her that? They thought her stuck up for not agreeing to marry anyone who deigned to give her attention. They thought her self-righteous for not making amends for luring Georgie to his death. They thought her a soiled dove for giving herself to Georgie, though she had done nothing of the kind.

To face that same disgust in a foreign country? To navigate other men like Georgie or his father, who thought of her as something to be used and tossed aside? To live her life in constant fear as she already did? Is that why Ben had been kind to her? Did he agree with Frieda? Did Agnes? Did hearing her shameful story last night only give them another reason to cast her to the wolves?

If she didn't get away, get out of this house, she might faint. Then what would they do to her? She'd have no control over how they treated her. No, she'd fight. She wouldn't let them use her. Unseeing, she stumbled toward the door.

"Eleanor, wait." Ben.

"Go away!" The words emerged as if shouted from another mouth. She had to escape before they forced her to do something she didn't want to do. Before Ben lured her to more danger than Georgie. This life Ben had was not something she could be a part of. It wasn't the cozy dream Amalie's idea had placed in her mind. She'd already battled a monster, there was no way she could ever face another.

Chapter Seventeen

Only Jim Taylor's hand on Ben's shoulder kept him from running after Eleanor, despite her protest. He'd never seen her so disoriented or pale. Even after last night's tears, she hadn't looked as ghostly as she had grown a moment ago.

"I'll keep her safe." Taylor patted Ben's back and disappeared outside.

"Freida is right." Otto switched to German. "That girl would be an asset to the cause. Think of the SS she could coerce into telling their secrets?"

"Not happening." Ben glared at his friend. Did the man not see Eleanor's distress at the very idea? Even if Ben didn't understand the cause of her reaction, he wouldn't let her be disparaged.

"We do a lot of unsavory things in times like these, Ben." Otto's tone softened, and Ben couldn't disagree. "We smuggle and lie, we break the law, but we save innocents that way because otherwise they would die."

Ben dropped his chin. Smuggling and lying were child's play compared to what Ben had done to save innocents like Eleanor and Amalie, and others.

"Is it the child?" Freida pointed her chin toward Amalie as she rocked her own boy. "I thought the woman was unmarried, but I won't separate a child from her mother."

"*Eleanor* is unmarried. Amalie is the orphan daughter of a mutual friend of Otto and mine."

Amalie crossed her arms, apparently not fond of being talked about. Hiram whispered something to her, but they stayed quiet enough Ben couldn't hear their exchange other than that they'd switched to English.

"If *Eleanor* is unmarried, then she should go to Germany." Heda spoke for the first time, crossing her arms with a similar attitude to Amalie. "We all must make sacrifices, or cruelty wins."

She was right, yet ...

"I can see you're worried for the child, and perhaps Eleanor has grown fond of her, and fears for her as well." Frieda adjusted the sleeping Max in her arms and kissed the top of his head. "I can take the girl with me. She'll be safe so you and Eleanor can concentrate on rescuing more children and their mothers from Germany."

"I will not go!" Amalie jumped from her chair.

"Hush, child." Agnes came to her side. "The adults—"

Amalie stomped her foot. "No!"

Ben knelt before her. "We want you to be safe, Amalie."

She threw her arms around his neck, reverting to muffled German as she pressed her face into his shoulder. "Don't make me leave, Ben. I don't want to leave you."

"Oh, dear one." Ben hugged her close. "I'm not good at being a father, and you would be much safer far from here."

"You don't have to be afraid." Frieda's motherly gentleness soaked her words. "My sister and I will be like aunts to you, Amalie. We will keep you safe so Ben and Eleanor can fight this battle for us."

"It's the right thing, Ben," Otto said from behind him, "and you know it."

Ben wished to deny it, but couldn't. Hadn't he said a similar thing to Taylor just that morning? He had to be as strong for Amalie as he did for Eleanor. He was not the right person for them. Surely he wouldn't worry as much if they were together.

He gently set Amalie on her own two feet, drying her tears with his thumb. "They are right, Amalie. You and Eleanor should go with Max and his mama and aunt."

Amalie's shoulders fell, then anger sparked in her eyes, and she pushed him away. "I won't." Then she spun away, darted between the grown-ups, and dashed out the door, all before Ben could catch his balance.

"Stay here." Hiram took his coat and a handful of others, and followed the little girl out the door.

Ben watched them, wanting to go after them. But Hiram and Taylor would keep his girls safe. *His girls.* Yeah, they were and always would be. But duty and calling, the saving of innocent lives ... He couldn't have his girls and fulfill the mission God had given him. His soul was already tarnished with the blood of those he'd killed, he couldn't—

"She's a feisty child." Heda didn't sound impressed.

"She's hurting." Frieda shrugged and kissed Max's head again.

"You know her parents wouldn't want her in danger, Ben." Otto pulled out two kitchen chairs and motioned the women into them. "If we can stop this downward march, it'll be over before too long, and you can be reunited. But if we don't stop what the Nazi Party is doing, it's only going to get worse. Deep in your heart, you know that."

Ben paced to the chair where Eleanor had been sitting. Her flowers and tea left on the side table. He glanced up and spoke in English. "Agnes, you have yet to voice an opinion."

"All I'll say," she said, but the glint in her eye said it wasn't all she was thinking by any stretch, "is that you are an important part of a necessary wheel to rescue innocent people, innocent children, from those who wish to do them harm. Whether because of their nationality, their disability, their ... whatever other arbitrary reason these men have deemed imperfect."

"She is right, Ben." Otto leaned his palms on the back of a chair.

Ben sighed. "I agree that Amalie must go with you, Frieda. Whether Eleanor does as well is up to her. She is my friend and must deliver news of me back to my family. Our task is not one she's agreed to take up."

"She should." Heda huffed. "This Third Reich is not just our problem. It is a cancer that will spread. If you doubt me, don't. My brother-in-law believes so profoundly in an Aryan race that he disowned his own son and stole that sweet baby away from his mother."

Frieda bit her lip and bent as if she could cocoon her son from the reality of Heda's words. Nor could Ben dispute them. Frieda and Max had experienced the ugliness of what was happening in Germany firsthand, and Heda was right to be worried that the cancer would grow. Even one of the British papers warned of that just a few weeks ago. If allowed to go unchecked ... Ben shuddered to think what atrocities lay ahead.

"Enough conversation for now. You have traveled far." Agnes switched the conversation back to English, safeguarding the secret of her German fluency. He wondered if Amalie had figured it out yet.

"Agnes is correct again. It is time to rest, then we will make plans." Ben glanced around, though he didn't understand why. Looking for Eleanor, though she wasn't here? His unease grew. "I need to go find Eleanor and Amalie."

Agnes gave an approving nod, then returned to the stove. Before he had finished buttoning his coat and donning his hat, she had prepared a sack of provisions. "Hiram thought to grab coats, but they've been gone for a while, and we both know the weather can change quickly. Be careful."

Weather wasn't the only reason he'd need care.

He thanked Agnes, then set out from the house to the road. Did they go left toward town or right toward the cliffs? If Amalie and Hiram had followed Eleanor, he would find all four to the left.

Following Heather Wynd, he passed the other houses on the row. Numbers eight, nine, ten. There were fourteen houses in all, and the fourteenth was the biggest. Owned by a family who gained their wealth in shipping, rumor had it the private residence boasted eight bedrooms and sweeping lawns. Ben hadn't been on the property to see for himself. Most neighbors of that echelon kept well away from him.

Past number fourteen, the ground rose through the forested area that surrounded this section of the loch. He paused. Had they gone left toward Creag An Larlain or continued straight up through the forest to the rocky rise above?

It wasn't a mountain in the way they thought of them back in Montana, but it was still a climb with significant elevation. More concerning was the warning Agnes had issued. The weather could change at a moment's notice, and already the clouds had descended despite the sun of the morning. There had been plenty of rain lately, and that could make way for mudslides.

Instinct told Ben that Eleanor wouldn't have traveled far from the Loch and the path where they'd discovered Taylor yesterday, so he veered right. And, if Amalie and Hiram were with them, they would be able to direct them to Ben's hut, which was past the trees, though nowhere near any of the cairns atop the rocky rise. Yes, if all four had met up, he should find them all this way.

Fingers of mist crept down from the higher elevation like the fear creeping down Ben's neck. No, that was the feeling he got when someone watched him. Had the other bounty hunter arrived? Was Ben leading more danger right toward the two girls he cared most about in the world? Or would he arrive in time to warn them away, not just from the cliffs around Loch Ness, but also from him?

Ben glanced over his shoulder and, seeing no sign of anyone, quickened his pace. He needed to find Eleanor and Amalie and make sure they were safe, then get them on a boat back to America as quickly as possible. No matter the cost, no matter how much they hated him for it. There was no limit to what else he'd give up for them, including his heart, his soul, and even his life.

Chapter Eighteen

Eleanor snuggled more deeply into the coat Hiram had brought her. She suspected that, if she showed signs of hypothermia, Jim Taylor would haul her back to the cottage whether she wanted to go or not.

Thankfully, neither Hiram nor Mr. Taylor had scolded her for allowing emotion to cloud her judgment. She shouldn't have run off into unfamiliar territory.

"The clouds hide everything." Amalie snuggled herself more securely against Eleanor's side. They sat on a rocky knob high enough to see over the trees that circled Loch

Ness. Or they would have been high enough to see if the clouds hadn't sunk so low.

Eleanor sighed and glanced toward where Hiram and Jim Taylor sat—close enough to respond to danger, but far enough that she and Amalie could talk without the men hearing them. She appreciated their respectful silence. Having Ben and the others telling her what to do, what to sacrifice, without understanding the fear she harbored, had unnerved her.

"We should probably go back." Even if returning to Agnes's cottage was the last thing she wanted to do right now.

"No." Amalie rested her head on Eleanor's shoulder. "Ben will send us to America."

She'd been surprised Amalie and Hiram had caught up to her and Mr. Taylor. Grateful, too, since Hiram had brought their jackets. Using her best English, Amalie had spilled the entire story of what happened back at the cabin, and how Ben agreed with Otto and the other women that Amalie should go to America.

"Do you want to go to America?" Amalie asked, a tremor in her question.

"It is my home." It seemed decisions had to be made, and neither she nor Amalie wanted others to make those decisions for them. With so many opinions swirling and seasoned with such emotion, Amalie couldn't discern the best course of action.

Amalie shifted closer. "Is it rainy like this at your home?"

"No. You can see the blue sky for miles and miles, it seems. We have mountains, too. Real ones. They're so big, some have snow hats all year round." She searched the tree line for signs of Ben. Would he track them down? Did he agree that Eleanor should go back to America without him? Or did he, too, think she should face another destructive man for the German cause?

"One summer, mama and papa took me to mountains like that," Amalie said, seemingly oblivious to Eleanor's inner turmoil. Good. "The Bayerische Alpen, they are called. They are all the way in the south of Deutschland."

"I'd like to see those someday." Eleanor wrapped her arm around Amalie's shoulder and rested her cheek against the little girl's blonde head. "We have much in common, don't we, dear one?"

She nodded and counted on her fingers. "We like mountains. We like Ben. Ben saved us from bad men. We have no mama and papa."

Eleanor's heart cracked at the dispassionate way Amalie listed their similarities.

Amalie plucked a pebble from near her knee. "If Ben makes me go to America, I want to go with you."

Surety hit instantly. "I wouldn't have it any other way." No matter what anyone else said, or whether it meant bringing her back to Montana, or staying here with Agnes, or following her to another country all together—she would never leave this child alone.

Eleanor had nothing drawing her back to America. Sure, she'd miss Cora's friendship, but never having to face Mr. Brown again sounded lovely. She'd endured enough disapproval, she could manage it again to stay with Amalie. This little girl would be her mission now, wherever that would lead.

But it didn't solve the dilemma about Ben.

She again glanced over at Hiram and Taylor. They appeared to be in serious conversation. Concern had her taking in their surroundings more carefully. In her emotional haze, she had forgotten the possible danger to

Ben.. Is that why Ben didn't want her and Amalie near him? Did he think they would be in danger when he was the target?

In that case, why was everyone worried about what country she and Amalie lived in when they should be focused on keeping Ben alive? As much as she had no desire to return to Agnes's cabin and face Otto and the others right now, she couldn't be selfish and hope Ben would come looking for her. A pang struck her. That's what one of the German ladies had called her. Perhaps she was right.

"We should get back." Eleanor rose, but Amalie did not. "We need to get back to Ben."

Amalie crossed her arms. "I do not want to talk to him."

Eleanor cast a helpless glance at the men, who had risen when she did. She understood Amalie's frustration, felt it herself.

"Ready to head back?" Mr. Taylor asked as he and Hiram approached.

"Not really." Eleanor glanced at Amalie who gave no doubt as to her answer, yet she felt compelled to explain. "She doesn't want to talk to Ben right now."

"Neither do you." Hiram bumped her arm.

True. "I'm worried if Ben tries to find us, he'll be in danger."

"Kind of you, considering." Mr. Taylor offered a closed smile. Did he disagree with how she'd been treated? "I saw no signs of anyone around the cabin or anyone following us. And sitting up here we have an open view. I don't think you need to worry for your safety, or Amalie's. Though it is getting colder and the air is getting damp. We should get to shelter, but it doesn't need to be at Agnes's house."

Amalie's scowl lightened.

"Where else can we go?" A raindrop splashed her cheek.

Mr. Taylor glanced at the darkening clouds. "I was going to suggest the boardinghouse where I'm staying, but it's all the way in Bieldfell. Not far by Montana standards, but we'll be drenched and you don't have spare clothes."

"Ben's cabin is closest." Hiram held up a hand to stop the protests forming in Eleanor's mind and on Amalie's face. "He won't be there."

"And he won't mind us staying there without him." Mr. Taylor waved them toward the trees. "We need to hurry if we don't want to get caught in a downpour."

Eleanor took Amalie's hand and followed Hiram. The trees sheltered them from the increasing rain. Despite her feelings, Eleanor kept hoping Ben would find them. It made no sense.

Or perhaps it did. Ben had always been her protector. She trusted him, felt safe with him. Even when he frustrated her, which had happened numerous times during their youth, usually because she went off on an adventure he hadn't been keen on. Sixteen years later, their friendship still held the same friction.

Eleanor's damp hair stuck to her neck, and her wet dress grew heavy. Mud spattered their clothes as they descended the hill. Mr. Taylor hurried them along until Hiram stopped them at the edge of a pasture filled with heavily woolen sheep. Shearing season must be soon.

"That's Ben's hut." Hiram pointed to the small wooden structure in the center of the field. "Rain is coming down. Let's make it quick."

Eleanor adjusted her grip on Amalie's hand and lifted her skirt for better speed. It had been ages since she'd run in the rain, but a thrill of excitement dashed through her as they took their first steps out of the trees.

Once upon a time, she and Ben had gone on rainy adventures. She wished he was here now, without the threat of danger or the worries about innocent lives being harmed in other countries. She wished Georgie Brown had never cornered her that day sixteen years ago and that Ben hadn't run from the accusations of murder. Then maybe they'd still be in Montana, happily—

Her steps stumbled to a stop as they rounded the corner of Ben's hut. The door was open. Had the rain done that, or something more sinister?

Hiram took Amalie's hand, and Mr. Taylor pushed them toward the side of the house, drawing a pistol from his hip. The men exchanged silent communication that Eleanor understood. Hiram would defend them while Mr. Taylor looked inside.

Amalie pressed against Eleanor. Sheep watched while the rain drenched them.

Mr. Taylor aimed his pistol at the opening, then kicked the door fully out of his way. "Hands up!"

Hiram yanked them away from the building and back toward the trees. They had to get back to Ben. She and Amalie didn't need to leave Scotland. Ben did.

Chapter Nineteen

B EN SPUN, FINGER ON the trigger of his revolver.
"Taylor."

The man huffed out a breath, but didn't holster his weapon. "The girls are with me."

"Bring them in." Ben lowered his weapon. "Whoever did this is gone."

Taylor whistled, waved, then stepped inside. "Whoa."

Yeah. Ben didn't have many belongings, but what little he had was now destroyed. Slashed, smashed, torn to bits. Not a chair, plate, cup or lantern had survived the intruder.

Taylor surveyed the damage. "I take it you suspect a human."

"Unlike back home, here in the Highlands, there aren't any large predators who would even be capable of this type of damage."

Taylor stepped halfway outside, watching. "You think someone local?"

"I'd take a gamble that it's another bounty hunter."

Taylor shot him a look. "The ladies are more likely to kick your shins right now, especially the little one. Eleanor at least wanted to make sure you're safe."

"Is he gone?" Hiram's low voice carried from outside.

"Yes." Taylor hesitated. "Ben's here."

Ben holstered his revolver and braced for the response to his presence. Then drew again when Taylor darted from the door. "Oh no, you don't, little lady."

"Get inside." Hiram pushed Eleanor into the dim interior and took sentry at the door.

Eleanor eyed him, lips pursed. Lips he had to drag his eyes from even though he wanted to kiss them. Ridiculous thought, considering the irritation in her face, but seeing his hut like this had shaken the truth loose. There would always be people who could fight the battle beside Otto, Frieda, and Heda, but who would fight for Eleanor? Who would protect her from a man who could destroy like this?

"Why aren't you at Agnes's house?" Eleanor tugged her soaked coat tighter across her shoulders.

"You need to get dry." Ben holstered his revolver again, and searched his hut. "I'd offer you a change of clothes, but they've been shredded. I'm not sure I trust the stove, he surely tampered with it."

"Ben." Eleanor's tone drew him back. "I don't care about the rain."

"Inside with you, Miss Amalie." Taylor carried her out of the rain and Hiram shut the door, washing the room in darkness.

"I don't have a working lantern." Ben rubbed his face. "Open the door so we can see one another, would you?"

Someone did as he asked.

"I'll watch outside." Taylor moved to the door.

"No." Hiram bared the door with his arm. "You work with these three on a plan. I'll keep watch."

Taylor nodded.

Hiram glanced around the man, then jerked his chin at Eleanor and Amalie. "Ben? Talk to them."

Taylor planted his hands on his belt. "Do you need to clear the air before we plan how to fake your death?"

Eleanor and Amalie's expressions would have been comical in another situation. Ben breathed out the tension coiled in his chest. "As soon as the rain lessens, we need to move locations. Let's get the plan in place, then we'll talk."

Eleanor relaxed, but Amalie stopped her foot. "I will not go to America."

Ben knelt in place. "I know. I'm sorry, Amalie. Your parents entrusted you to my care so however this plan works out, I'll take you with me."

Her anger faded and she clutched Eleanor's hand. "I want to stay with Eleanor, too."

Eleanor smiled, running her hand over Amalie's wet hair.

Ben swallowed. He didn't deserve it, but could there be any way this could be his little family? "Jim. What do we do?"

"Have a seat." Jim kicked at the broken remnants of Ben's home, clearing a space on the floor. "I thought of a plan last night, but since Ben here didn't want to hear it this morning, I'll explain it now. However, considering the developments of the afternoon, I suspect we'll need to adjust it."

Eleanor covered her feet with her skirt and let Amalie lean against her. "You want to fake Ben's death so Mr. Brown stops hunting for him?"

"How will that help Eleanor?" Ben sat, knees propping up his arms.

Taylor matched Ben's position. "The idea came to me when I overheard my landlady talking about the Loch Ness monster. If it capsizes your boat and you disappear, no one will question your supposed death."

"Monster?" Amalie scooted closer to Eleanor.

"We're not sure it's real." Taylor smiled at her. "And Ben wouldn't really die. It would be pretend so the bad men will think he is dead."

Amalie rested her head against Eleanor. "I wish my mama and papa could be pretend dead."

Ben dropped his head. To save other children like Amalie or fulfill his promise to her parents. An impossible choice that would leave him with guilt no matter which path he chose.

"What about us?" Eleanor asked, her voice rising, causing Hiram to peek into the partially open door. "If Ben is supposedly dead, what happens to me and Amalie? Do we return to Montana without him? Do we tell his grandparents he is dead? Are you expecting me to tell George Brown?"

Ben had no answer to her questions, but he'd caught something else she said. "You would take Amalie with you?"

Eleanor bristled, wrapping Amalie in a protective hug. "Absolutely. Whatever happens, the two of us stay together. We've decided that much."

"Good," Hiram grunted, then returned his attention outside.

"Ben?" Taylor raised his brows.

"So I supposedly die by a monster and the girls go back to my grandparents." He looked to Eleanor. "You'll tell them the truth? I can't bear to have them think I'm dead. I know you all will have to make a show of it, but—"

"You're going to make us all lie for you?" Eleanor snapped.

"I don't have a choice." Hopelessness settled across his shoulders, a feeling much worse than the guilt he felt over ending a life to save one. In that case, he had a choice. He always chose the innocent one, the one who needed a protector. "Or maybe I do. I'm choosing you and Amalie. I'm ending my life as I know it so you'll be free."

"Exactly." Eleanor kissed the top of Amalie's head. "Go with Mr. Taylor for a moment, dear one. I need to talk to Ben."

Amalie stood, but put her hands on Eleanor's cheeks to make her look at her. "You promise not to leave without me?"

"Yes." Eleanor copied Amalie. "I promise I will not leave without you. We go together no matter what."

Without protest, Amalie took Taylor's hand and the three stepped into the rain with Hiram.

"Perhaps those three should come inside, and we stand outside." Eleanor stood. "I'd suggest it, but you're the one in danger, so you should stay hidden."

Ben rose as well, but kept his distance. "May I speak first?"

"No." Eleanor faced him, rigid. "You're doing it again, Ben. You're taking our friendship into your own hands. Sixteen years ago, you disappeared to keep me safe. You would do it again and for the same reason."

"Absolutely." He risked a step closer. "I would do anything for you and Amalie."

Her shoulders relaxed a smidgen. "I know, Ben. You have the most noble of hearts."

"I don't know about that."

"I do." She decreased the distance between them. "You are willing to take on the guilt, shame, and pain of ending a life in order to save an innocent person. You gave up your home, your family—"

"My best friend."

"Yes, your best friend. All so that you could save me from Mr. Brown's wrath."

"And I'd do all of that again." Ben closed the space between them and grabbed her shoulders. "Don't you see, El?"

"I do, and that's why I refuse to let you do it again."

"I don't understand."

Her hand seared his chest as she laid her palm on his heart. "It's time you leave your reclusive ways. It's time you leave the guilt. You have done nothing to deserve that pain."

How Ben wanted to believe her. "But I've done such horrible things."

"You've killed people, yes." Eleanor didn't flinch. "But, Ben, you didn't murder them."

Ben blinked. "What's the difference?"

"One is evil. Against all that is good." She set her other hand on his chest. "But you, Ben? What you did was justified. Your actions saved and protected those who could not fight for themselves. Had you not pulled Georgie away from me, I have no doubt he would have shoved it deeper until I would have bled out in minutes."

Tears burned. "Don't relive this, El."

"You have to." She wrapped her fingers in his shirt. "You have to forgive yourself. You have to allow yourself to be vindicated. Ben, you did nothing wrong. It wasn't just reasonable, it was heroic. You're a hero. You're *my* hero."

Like the clanging of a jail's door sliding open, her words allowed him to breathe fresh air for the first time in sixteen years. Shame and guilt fell from his shoulders. No longer did the clouds and mist obscure his soul from God.

He pulled Eleanor into an embrace, trapping her hands between them, and lifted his eyes to the ceiling. No longer did the roof feel as if it limited him. Chains had fallen, scales lay scattered like the broken destruction of his belongings. And a verse, long shadowed, emerged as if on the cool, rain-scented breeze.

There is therefore now no condemnation to them which are in Christ Jesus.

The mantle God had laid on him wasn't because his hands were stained with blood, but because God had given him a spirit of justice and charged him with defending the innocent and protecting those without the strength to fend off those intent on evil deeds.

"Ben?" Eleanor pushed against him.

He eased his hold enough to rest his forehead on hers. "I love you, El."

She gave a sharp inhale.

He plunged on. "I always have, but I didn't know what that meant or how to love you as you deserved. I'm sorry I left you. I'm sorry you had to face Brown and the townspeople and all the pain alone. Forgive me, El. Please."

She nodded. "Y—"

Such relief crashed through him that he captured her mouth in a kiss before she could finish the word. Whatever tension had remained seeped out so she leaned into him, kissing him with as much longing and desperation as he felt churning within.

This woman. How had he thought leaving was the right thing to do? Sixteen years ago, or now?

He pulled away. Eleanor blinked, unsteady on her feet. He kissed her again, quick and sure. Then he grabbed Eleanor's hand and tugged her toward the door. "Taylor, it's not just my death we're faking. I'm taking my girls with me."

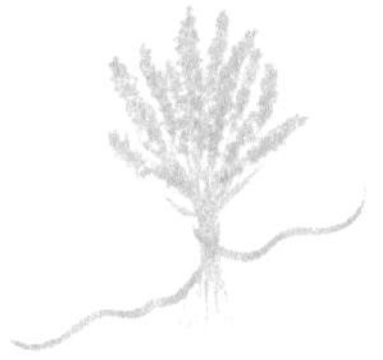

Chapter Twenty

NERVES SKITTERED LIKE SPIDERS over Eleanor's skin. Today would end her life as she knew it and begin a whole new one. She'd give up her name, her past, to join Ben in the mission to help rescue others like Amalie. Not only that, she'd be Ben's wife and Amalie's mother. Roles she'd given up.

Eleanor squeezed the little girl's hand as they followed Mr. Taylor out of Beildfell. To the locals, it would look as if he were spiriting Eleanor and Amalie away from Bieldfell and Ben in the early hours of the morning.

Amalie gave her a brave smile. She'd been through so much change in the last couple months, this would hopefully be the last. Once they settled in The Netherlands, there would be no more moving about. They'd be a family. A family!

Mr. Taylor stopped at a fork in the road at the edge of Bieldfell and looked first at Eleanor, then Amalie. "Seems an appropriate place to ask one more time: are you sure about this?"

"I'm sure." Eleanor huffed out the nerves that tangled her insides. She was sure. She had nothing left in Blue Spruce. A few friends, yes, but Cora had family of her own there. Eleanor had been ostracized, gossiped about, and had no gentlemen awaiting her return. Her future was with Ben.

"Nerves are good." Mr. Taylor patted her arm, then nudged his chin to the side. "They help to sell what we're doing."

A knot of ladies chatted out of hearing, but their obvious glances told Eleanor she, Amalie, and Mr. Taylor were the object of their conversation. Would she ever be free of tattletale biddies? Truly, even being a wife and mother might not free her of that, but she could dream, right?

"And how about you, Amalie?" Mr. Taylor squatted to be at her level. "Is this the path you wish to go down? If not, say the word and I'll change the plan. And I know Eleanor will go wherever you desire."

Amalie shifted closer to Eleanor and her heart twanged. If Amalie changed her mind, Eleanor would go with her, even if it meant leaving Ben behind. Not that Ben would let them go without him. But they might not have a choice. Still, this little girl had been through so much.

Eleanor bent to match Mr. Taylor's height. "He's right, Amalie. It's okay if you have second thoughts."

She leaned her head against Eleanor's arm. "I want to stay with you and Ben. I want you to be my new mama and papa."

"Oh, sweetheart." Eleanor kissed her temple.

Amalie turned wide blue eyes up at her. "You won't let me forget my real mama and papa, right?"

"We will talk of them whenever you wish so you will always feel them here." Eleanor tapped Amalie's chest. "Your papa was a dear friend of Ben's, so he can tell you stories. And I want to learn all about your mama and papa. Is that alright with you?"

Amalie nodded, her face changing from one of trepidation to excitement. She bounced on her toes. "I'm ready now. Can we see the boat?"

Eleanor exchanged a smile with Mr. Taylor, her own trepidation lessening with Amalie's change in mood. Once they made it through the next hour or so, they'd be free. Ben would be free.

"Okay." Mr. Taylor rose, as did Eleanor. "Then let's set this plan into—"

"Thank goodness I caught you." Agnes hustled toward them, making a big show of waving them down. The gossips nearby openly stared, and a few more passersby stopped to watch the scene unfolding. This wasn't part of the plan.

"Agnes." Mr. Taylor's voice held a warning.

Agnes gave a subtle wink, then spoke loudly enough their growing audience could hear. "I had to thank you for revealing what kind of man that Ben was. Pulling the wool over an old woman's eyes. Humph."

Eleanor bit her cheek.

"Hiram is distracting that man so you can get these sweet girls away from him. You'll have to hurry though. Hiram can't delay him for long. Ben fancies himself in love."

"You're not helping," Eleanor hissed in a desperate attempt to stop a blush.

Agnes slapped an envelope against Mr. Taylor's chest as pink rose in her cheeks. "Would you deliver this to his employer when you return the girls to their home? Hiram has decided to, um, stay here in Bieldfell. There's a letter of reference in there for you, too, so don't be a stranger, Mr. Taylor. We want to see you again."

"Wait." Mr. Taylor shook his head. "Why is he staying?"

Agnes turned bright red. "The man's proposed."

Eleanor laughed. She couldn't help it. "I wondered why he entrusted me to Mr. Taylor after seeing me here himself. I never thought he'd give up his bachelor ways."

"Yes, yes. Apparently he's ... well, he's smitten." Agnes fanned herself. "Goodness, this wasn't why I wanted to catch up with you."

"Is this real," Mr. Taylor whispered, "or are you acting?"

"I'm quite surprised by it myself, Mr. Taylor."

Eleanor took Agnes's hands. "I'm happy for you. Hiram is a good man."

"Herr Hiram asked me about you, Fraulein Agnes," Amalie said. "I told him you watch him like he watched you."

Poor Agnes's cheeks flamed an even more brilliant red. "He's just so … so … nevermind. Here, Eleanor. This is our parting gift to you. It's wrapped well in oilskin and won't be damaged aboard your ship home."

Eleanor sobered at the reminder of their upcoming plan and took the packet from Agnes. "What is this?"

Agnes lowered her voice. "It's everything you need, all the paperwork for your new life."

"Ben said to trust you to handle this part, but everything?" Mr. Taylor kept his voice low as well. "Birth and marriage records, identification, travel visas? How did you get all of that so fast?"

Agnes gave him a sympathetic pat. "I put this in motion long ago."

Eleanor put the packet into her knapsack. "I thought Cora found you."

"Oh, dear one. If I hadn't wanted you to find Ben, you wouldn't have. Why do you think it took sixteen years? It was time. And this little girl needed you."

Eleanor absorbed the news, the timeline, and had no doubt—in hindsight—that this crafty woman had done exactly what she'd said.

Agnes removed a gold chain from her pocket, the Star of David dangling from one end. "This is for you, Amalie. You're going to a new life where no one will know you were born to Jewish parents. But do not forget the God of your heritage. He is watching over you and will care for you as He does the sparrow and the flowers." She clasped the necklace around Amalie's neck and Amalie tucked it beneath her collar, tears shining.

"We need to go." Mr. Taylor tucked the envelope Agnes had given him into his inner coat pocket. "Thank you, Agnes. I will see you again soon."

"Indeed you will." Agnes hugged Eleanor, then Amalie. "Godspeed, dear ones."

Eleanor blinked back tears as she clasped Amalie's hand once again. This was it. There would be no going back.

"We need to hurry before the fog lifts from the loch. It will provide cover from those watching on shore." Mr.

Taylor took her elbow and led them toward the water where a wooden fishing boat waited.

Only, Mr. Taylor had prepared a leak that would strand them close enough from shore where they could be seen to capsize, but far enough that those watching would be unable to save them. Ben would appear in time to save them, only to fail. She hated that part, that Ben would forever be seen as a failure, not the hero she knew him to be. But for this to work, they had to all appear to die.

Eleanor's hands shook as Mr. Taylor helped her, then Amalie, into the boat. She and Ben had grown up swimming the rivers and lakes around Blue Spruce. The cold water of the loch wouldn't faze either of them, now, seeing that the source of their Montana rivers were the mountain snowpacks. Amalie said she also knew how to swim, but there was still an inherent danger in this whole plan. Nature was unpredictable and none of them had yet seen the bounty hunter who had destroyed Ben's cabin.

Mr. Taylor untied the mooring rope and took up the oars.

"Why is that man staring at us?" Amalie asked as she tucked herself into Eleanor's side as they sat in the stern.

"What man?" Eleanor searched the shore. There was an uncomfortable number of people milling about.

"Black coat, newsboy hat." Mr. Taylor pulled back on the oars, launching them away from shore. "I couldn't get a good look at his face, but if it's who I think it is ..."

"It's the other bounty hunter?" Eleanor tightened her hold on Amalie. "Did we or did we not want him to see us?"

"I did before I thought it would be this particular bounty hunter." Mr. Taylor's muscles rippled as he worked the oars, increasing their speed as well as their distance from shore. "No one knows his real name since he operates as a ghost most of the time. People call him BlackJack and he's more assassin than bounty hunter. Not a man you want to cross."

"Will he hurt us like that man hurt my mama and papa?" Amalie asked and Eleanor wished she could take away Amalie's heartache.

Mr. Taylor's jaw ticked. "Neither Ben nor I will let that happen, but it's important you know the risks ahead. Amalie, you must do everything Eleanor tells you to do. And Eleanor, if something happens to both me and Ben, get to the meeting point and get word to Agnes."

Eleanor nodded, fear closing her throat. This had to succeed. They had to get away from Brown's vengeance once and for all. Forest crags rose up on either side of the loch, creating a gauntlet they'd need to traverse. Mist hung low and menacing. Eleanor shivered.

Please, God, keep us safe. All of us.

Chapter Twenty-One

FROM A ROCKY OUTCROPPING above the eastern bank of Loch Ness, Ben watched his little family leave shore. A family. His family. How had he—a man accused of murder, whose hands had killed, who hid in the shadows—come to have such an incredible woman and child love him?

Hiram clapped his shoulder. "You ready for this?"

"I hate putting them in danger." Ben stared at the boat through the mist, willing it along, knowing it would begin taking on water any moment, then Eleanor would signal his doomed rescue. He wished he could be in the boat with them, assuring their safety. "Was this the right decision?"

"You know Brown won't stop until you're dead." Hiram shrugged. "Those girls have no family to leave behind and they want to spend their lives with you."

Humbling, oh so humbling, that fact. "Will I be a good enough husband and father, Hiram? My own father was a cruel, horrible man."

"But your grandfather is not."

Ben snorted. "I was scared of him most of my life."

"Yet you resemble him in more ways than one." Hiram patted his shoulder, then dropped his hand. "Agnes prepared your paperwork, including a marriage license. But do me a favor when you stop in Gretna Green. Actually get married."

Ben rubbed his neck. "How do you know about that?"

"Never you mind, son. I know this is all clandestine, but Eleanor deserves a real marriage."

"I love her, Hiram." His eyes never strayed from Eleanor's distant figure. She had begun baling water. It was almost time. "We might live under new identities, but that won't change how I feel about her."

"Good." Hiram crossed his arms. "You're a good man, Ben. I'm proud of who you've become."

Ben's gaze shot to Hiram for only a second, but it was enough to see the emotion on the old cowboy's face. "This isn't goodbye. Eleanor, Amalie, and I will be living on the Scheldt River. You and Agnes should visit."

He felt Hiram's stare. "How do you know about me and Agnes?"

Ben stifled a grin. "You might be old, but I can spot love when it bites a man."

Hiram punched his shoulder. "Took you sixteen years to realize it had bitten you."

"Nope. I knew it all along." Ben double checked that his gear was sufficiently hidden out of sight, and that his knife was securely fashioned to his belt. "I just wasn't mature enough to know what to do about it."

"If you say so." Hiram grunted.

"I say— There's another boat." Ben inched forward, careful not to reveal his hiding spot.

"Binoculars." Hiram slapped them into Ben's stomach.

He lifted them and focused on the single figure in the other boat. "A man. Oh no."

"The other bounty hunter." Hiram snatched the binoculars. "That's BlackJack. Heard of him, and none of it good. What are you waiting for? Go."

"I can't." Ben held himself in place. Barely. "I have to trust Eleanor. She'll give me the signal to rescue her. Too early and this whole plan implodes."

Hiram's silence churned Ben's stomach. He couldn't lose Eleanor. Not again.

Ben pinned his eyes on the woman he loved. She had Amalie held close. Taylor stood to confront the bounty hunter. "I feel so helpless."

Hiram, again, stayed silent.

The crowd gathering on the south shoreline did not. Shouts drew his attention to them. He couldn't make out the identity of anyone in particular through the haze, but several pointed toward the exchange happening on the water. No. *Under* the water.

"Hiram." Ben watched a black shadow circle under the boats. This couldn't be happening. The monster was real?

Eleanor glanced toward where he'd promised to wait for her, looking for him, yet gave no rescue signal. Taylor exchanged his oar for a rifle, attention split between the bounty hunter who nervously watched the water and the behemoth beneath them. Worse, like observing a gothic tableau, Ben watched as BlackJack pointed his pistol at the water and fired.

The sound unglued Ben's feet and he took off toward the water. Eleanor and Amalie screamed, their echoes bouncing off the half-concealed cliffs that overlooked the loch. The beast beneath the water rammed into the boats, knocking Taylor to his knees with a splash—the boat had taken on that much water already? The other bounty hunter maintained his balance and again fired at the water.

"Stop shooting!" Ben waved his arms in the air as the shadowed beast took aim at the boats again. Their plan had disintegrated. No more faking death. His girls needed a real, life-saving rescue. "Eleanor, jump!"

The cacophony from the shouting onlookers, Hiram's words from beside him, all blended into the background as the beast struck the boats again, sending the one with his little family bucking through the air.

Eleanor and Amalie were tossed into the water. Taylor landed in the BlackJack's boat, a calculated tumble, if Ben had his guess, and BlackJack fired off another round into the air as he fell on his backside.

Ben dove into the water, careless of the monsters below and above. Both could kill him or his girls, but the safety of his family came before his own. Powerful strokes sent him toward Eleanor, only she pushed Amalie toward him and turned back to the sinking boat.

"El!" Ben reached for the wide-eyed girl. Amalie clung to his neck, feet drawn as close to the surface of the water as she could manage.

"Go. Get her to shore." Eleanor hauled herself into the boat and Ben had no choice but to obey. The faster he delivered Amalie to Hiram, the quicker he could return to Eleanor. What could be so all-fired important that she would risk her life?

Amalie clung to him as he swam back the way he'd come. He half expected a bullet in the back, yet was able to hand Amalie to Hiram without injury. Turning, he realized why. Taylor was attempting to wrestle the pistol from BlackJack, and cheers erupted from the crowd.

Feeding on their enthusiasm, he swam back to Eleanor, who had retrieved a knapsack. He was only halfway back to her when she attempted to slide back into the water.

"Eleanor, stop!" Ben swam faster. The boat, nearly three-quarters full, would tip, sending the water gushing over her head and plunge her down to where the beast waited below. She needed his help.

BlackJack leveled a punch to Taylor's chin, knocking him on his backside. Recognition lit in the man's dark eyes as he caught sight of Ben powering through the water. His mouth tipped into a smile as he aimed his pistol at Ben.

"Don't!" Eleanor shouted, drawing the man's aim and stopping Ben's heart.

Taylor landed a foot to the man's knees, knocking him sideways as he fired. Eleanor ducked, lost her balance, and tumbled into the water. The boat tipped, just as Ben feared. Water sloshed over her head and the boat covered her.

Ben dove, aiming for where she flailed in the water, her feet tangled in her skirt. The dark form of the monster circled below her. A bullet, two, tore past him, whether they hit him or the beast, or sank to the bottom of the loch, he didn't know.

His only thought: save Eleanor.

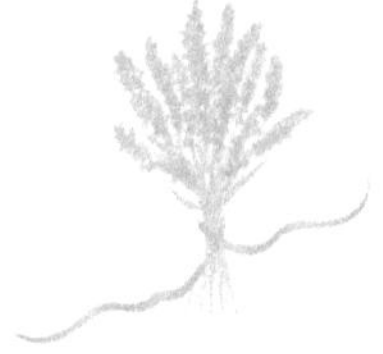

Chapter Twenty Two

Eleanor sank into the loch without enough air in her lungs. Water pushed her deeper despite clawing upward.

A bullet, two, three, shot past her and she barely held in a scream. The sea creature darted around, then sped toward her.

She tried to move, tried to escape. Panic threatened.

Then Ben was there.

Strong and solid, he wrapped his arm around her waist and pulled her against his chest. Not up like she wanted, but away from the beast and its rapid ascent. It flew up like a bird of prey, and crashed through the sunken boat on its way to the surface.

Then Ben was in motion. He hauled her upwards, arm around chest, until she broke the surface. She gulped at the air, her lungs burning. Water and hair covered her face and she wiped it clear. Cheers erupted around them. She looked for the beast, for Taylor, for the bounty hunter.

"Ben!" Taylor shouted. "Look out!"

Ben pushed her away as a pistol fired. Again her legs caught in the cloth of her dress as she spun. Taylor and BlackJack were in the water, too, fighting over the pistol, their boat and oars floating nearby.

"Ben!" Where had he gone?

"El." He appeared behind her, laid a kiss on her cheek, then, before she realized what he was about, he sliced her skirt, freeing her legs. "Go. I'll meet you in Gretna. I promise."

Without waiting for a response, he gave her push, then swam for the bobbing boat, shoving it toward Taylor and BlackJack as another gunshot chipped a chunk out of the hull near Ben's head.

Eleanor stifled a scream, frozen. What should she do? Amalie needed her, but she couldn't leave Ben.

"El! Swim!" Ben shouted.

Then she heard Hiram, and the crowd calling the same. In the next instant, the whale-like monster crashed through the remains of the boat, sending splinters of wood flying into the air. Eleanor put her head into the water and swam toward Amalie as hard as she could.

It seemed forever before Hiram helped her out of the water and Amalie jumped into her arms. Still kneeling on the rocky shore, Eleanor looked back, searching for Ben.

The water had stilled. The crowd had gone silent.

Amalie sobbed against Eleanor's chest. Hiram squeezed her shoulder.

Come on, Ben.

Jim Taylor bobbed to the surface. A cheer from the crowd. Then BlackJack rose, too. And still everyone waited. And waited.

"Ben?" Amalie whispered.

Eleanor's heart hiccuped.

Mr. Taylor met her gaze across the water. *Go,* he mouthed. Her heart cracked.

"Let's go before BlackJack catches sight of us." Hiram helped her and Amalie up the cliff, a feat she couldn't have accomplished alone with how cold and numb she felt, both inside and out.

The plan had been to fake their deaths. Had it partially worked? Or was Ben really … Eleanor shook her head. She wouldn't believe it. Couldn't.

Hiram paused long enough to shoulder a pack, then hurried them onward. "I'll see you to the place where Ben planned to have you change from your wet clothes. Then you two get to Gretna Green."

Their meeting place.

Eleanor clutched his arm. "You think he survived?"

Hiram's jaw tightened. "Agnes and I will take care of things here. Get to Gretna Green. I'll meet you there in a couple days."

Eleanor nodded. If he arrived and Ben didn't, then they'd put a different plan in place. One that didn't include the man she loved. Had she told him she loved him? The past twenty-four hours had been a blur.

Neither she nor Amalie spoke the rest of the day other than out of absolute necessity. Hiram parted ways with them at the cave where they donned warm, dry clothes, then Eleanor and Amalie trekked north.

She didn't take note of the name of the town they came to, the scenery they passed, nor the critters that raced away from them. She cared for nothing but to get Amalie onto the train, then reach Gretna Green, and not fall apart when Amalie needed her to remain strong.

The hours blended one into the next, held together with a fragile thread of hope. Amalie leaned on her, but they both wanted Ben. The idea of going on without him? The whole point of faking their deaths had been so the three of them could be together. A family. She and Amalie had none save each other, and Ben.

"We have to hold onto hope, Amalie." Eleanor repeated the phrase whenever doubts threatened to undo her. She couldn't lose hold of her emotions. She had to keep herself together.

Arriving in Gretna Green, Eleanor followed Agnes's directions to a reputable boardinghouse. The older lady had thought of everything in that oilskin package. Securing it as she did had saved it from damage and Eleanor clung to the promise it provided. She had Ben's new identity, their marriage document, all they needed for their new lives.

Yet, night fell again without sign of him.

Their landlady seemed to have a sixth sense about these things, because she plied Eleanor and Amalie with sweet treats. Eleanor could barely manage a nibble, but with the lady's goading, Amalie found her appetite. She offered a bath, too, and kept Amalie busy in the kitchen as the afternoon waned.

By evening, even the fellow boarders seemed to understand that they waited for a loved one who might never arrive. Though Eleanor had kept quiet about Ben and his relationship to her and Amalie, Amalie had taken to calling her *ma*. Eleanor had suggested it since it sounded close to *mama*, but wouldn't suggest she was replacing the mother Amalie lost. Would she lose a second father, too?

Hope fractured as another night fell.

The second morning in Gretna Green, neither Eleanor nor Amalie could manage a smile, no matter the efforts the landlady and other boarders put forth. Eleanor expected Hiram now, and for the first time she didn't wish to see the man.

Snuggled on the bed, Amalie stayed by her side, and Eleanor read to her. Minutes turned to hours without sign of Hiram. Had she miscounted the days? Possible, considering the fog she'd lived in.

Tomorrow. Tomorrow would be a new day and she'd make a plan for herself and Amalie. They could survive this. They had to, for Ben. But tonight, after Amalie had fallen asleep, Eleanor would allow herself to grieve what could have been.

"Mrs. Van Berk?" Their landlady called up the stairs. "You have a gentleman caller."

Amalie sat up straight, knocking the book to the floor.

Eleanor took her hand. "Together."

Amalie nodded, biting her lip. It would be Ben or Hiram, hope or ... Eleanor steeled herself for the moments to come.

Down the steps they went, slowly at first, then more quickly, for Hiram wasn't at the bottom waiting for them. The dark-haired man with the beaming smile was one conjured from her youth. No more beard. Freshly trimmed hair. And a light in his eyes that Eleanor hadn't seen for over sixteen years.

"Pa!" Amalie squealed and launched herself off the staircase. Ben caught her midflight and spun her around, meeting Eleanor's eyes with tears in his own.

Then he set her down and stretched a hand to Eleanor. He swallowed, the bob evident without his beard covering his throat. The hint of a tattoo rose above the collar of his shirt. A dove with a branch in its mouth, if she wasn't mistaken. Eleanor stalled, unable to tear her gaze from the image. From that symbol of peace. Could that be theirs now?

"El?" Ben eased closer, concern replacing the joy.

But she couldn't speak past the emotions tumbling through her. The past days, she'd been the strong one, had hidden her fear, spoken of hope and the future. Trembling overtook her now as the events of the past days swept over her. Ben was here. He was safe, alive. Her knees buckled and she was in his arms.

"I'm here, El." He lifted her to his lap as he sat on a step and tucked her close. The tears came then. All the ones she'd stuffed away. Perhaps even those she'd held back for years.

Murmurs reached past her sobs, but she couldn't stop. Then Ben was carrying her to the parlor, closing the door behind them, and settling on the sofa.

"Shh." His voice roughed as he spoke. "The landlady offered to sit with Amalie for a moment. She knows how you've despaired of ever seeing me again."

"I was so afraid." She rested her head on his chest, revelling in the rhythmic beating of his heart.

"I'm sorry, my love. I knew it was my chance to stop Brown from hunting us. I stayed long enough to know I was declared missing and feared dead."

Hearing him utter such a phrase about himself struck her in a way that dried up tears, though her heart still felt bruised. "How did you escape?

Ben leaned back, leaving Eleanor perched on his lap. He ran his gaze over her, causing her cheeks to heat. She scrambled to her feet.

"You've become a rogue, sir."

He winked, then shook his head. "You are one incredible woman, El."

At a loss, she stood before him, arms flopping at her sides.

He patted the seat beside him and she obliged. "Do you believe it, I think that monster was my salvation. I suspect Ol' Ness was just trying to regain her peace and quiet. A recluse like me. Misunderstood and annoyed that someone was shooting at her."

Eleanor felt a smile tug at her mouth.

"She sent Taylor and BlackJack swimming for shore. While the crowds were distracted, I was able to slip away." Ben threaded his large fingers through hers. "Poor thing will be accused of murder now, for my sake. I don't envy her that fate. But perhaps rumor will guard her."

"Her?" Eleanor raised a brow. "Became friends, did you?"

"Of course. She's now another of my favorite gals. Like you." Ben considered Eleanor. "El, will you marry me?"

The question startled her so that she didn't quite know what to say. Of course they were to be married, and according to the certificate she carried, they already were. Plus, she was rather sure he'd asked her back in the cottage before the whole fake-death plan was set in place. But this was ... different.

He slipped off the sofa to kneel before her. "I made the biggest mistake of my life leaving Blue Spruce. I left the most incredible woman I have ever met. And I'll be honest: I've met a few. Not a one has ever matched your strength, your humility, your beauty. When you popped back into my life, I couldn't fathom that God would bring such a blessing to a man with blood on his hands."

Eleanor lifted the hand still entwined with hers to her heart.

"I love you, El. I want ours to be a real marriage. One built on love and truth and honesty, even while we operate in the shadows."

He tugged a ring from his pocket. It was a band of gold ivy. No diamonds, nothing flashy, but he opened her hand to lay it on her palm. Then he unbuttoned his left cuff to reveal the leaf tattoo she'd noted earlier.

"I got this the day I decided to join intelligence work. *I am the vine, ye are the branches: He that abideth in me, and I in him, the same bringeth forth much fruit: for without me ye can do nothing.* That goes for our marriage, too."

She nodded as words caught in her throat. Tears burned her nose, as if she had more to shed, but these were happy tears, not cleansing tears. She dashed one away. "I love you, Ben."

"And will you marry me?"

"Yes. Definitely y—"

She couldn't finish, seeing as how Ben kissed her. One hand on the sofa beside her, the other slipping behind her neck to pull her close as he still knelt before her. Eleanor set her palm against his clean-shaven cheek and kissed him back, drawing him to sit beside her.

Then whoo-ee did he kiss her! As if he were a man come home from a desert island. She clutched the ring, the leaves indenting her palm, leaving a temporary mark. Temporary pain that would be forgotten in a moment. Her future was in her hands now. As a mother, which she never dreamed she could be, to a daughter who needed a safe haven. As a wife to a man who sacrificed everything to fight for children, whom God loved but man tossed aside.

Ben slowed their kiss, then tucked her head under his chin, and helped her slip the ring onto her finger. Yes. She'd found her home, her hero. And no matter what name they took or place they lived, they would always be together.

Forever a family.

Epilogue

TWO MONTHS LATER ...

Jim Taylor galloped into the Blue Spruce, praying his days of planning would come to fruition. Dismounting in the center of town, he stood still a moment, inhaling the fresh Montana air. It was good to be back.

He filled his lungs once more, then set his sights on the buildings along Main Street. After having watched Eleanor for a number of months before she took off for Scotland, he had a good feel for the regular routines of those closest to her.

With that in mind, he knew Tuesdays were Town Days for Ben's grandparents and that the foreman, Silas Ward, always accompanied them. What Jim couldn't decide was whether he wanted to bait George Brown into the street. It might be best for him to overhear the news about Ben.

Jim slowed his pace as he led his horse past the bank, making sure one of Brown's goons saw him. Up ahead, he recognized the Orsons' wagon team waiting outside the general store. Yes, as awful as it was, making this a big scene would be the most beneficial.

Loitering until the old beast of a man escorted his beautiful wife out into the sunshine, Jim palmed the folded letter he carried from Ben. Took him a week of planning to make the stars align, but this had to be public or the ruse wouldn't work. There could be no doubt in Brown's mind.

The delay had also served to allow BlackJack to deliver his report first. Jim didn't care about the payment anymore, and he was sure BlackJack had told plenty of tales about Jim's change of loyalty. But Brown had predicted that, and now he needed to hear of Ben's supposed death from someone else.

Silas Ward settled his cowboy hat on his head as he followed his boss out of the store, his wife at his elbow and their child in her arms. Jim squared his shoulders to do what must be done.

"Mr. Orson?" He stepped forward. A quick glance about assured him that Brown's man had stepped onto the walk outside the bank, a couple of the loudest busybodies had paused outside the seamstress shop, and a general hum meant more curious onlookers would join them.

"I am." Caleb Orson stepped forward. He was a large man with massive shoulders and a bushy grey beard.

"You're Ben's grandfather." The similarities were remarkable.

"You found him?" Mrs. Orson grabbed her husband's arm, hope lighting her wrinkled features. Hushed whispers flared around them.

Jim forced his jaw to relax. "I have, ma'am."

She must have heard the regret in his voice. Tears came swiftly. Anger had Orson swelling to an even greater height. "You have proof?"

"He was there." Brown sauntered out of the bank. "Or so my man says. That true, Taylor?"

"Yes, sir." Jim stepped toward the Orsons. "He's a hero. The town of Beildfell watched as he risked his life to save a woman and child from the Loch Ness Monster."

The gossips gasped. Brown snorted.

"Our Ben?" Mrs. Orson swiped at her tears. "Our good boy."

Orson's nostrils flared and he stuck out his hand. "Thank you for telling us in person."

Jim shook, transferring the paper to Orson's palm. "He is finally at rest and has given his life for those who need a warrior to fight for them."

Orson gave a single nod, understanding in his eyes. "Let's go home, Love." He escorted his wife to the wagon, ignoring the women who chattered nearby. Jim didn't know the full contents of that letter, but Ben had decided to risk telling them the truth.

Mrs. Ward glanced between her husband and the Orsons. Ward gave a nod for her to go with them, then crossed his arms. "You couldn't have delivered that news in the privacy of their own home?"

Brown laughed and Jim let the embarrassment creep up his neck. "I'm sorry for it. No hard feelings?" He stuck out his hand.

Ward considered him a moment, then clasped his palm with a punishing grip.

Jim pulled him closer. "Punch me in the gut and tell Cora that Eleanor has a husband, a daughter, and her happily ever after."

Ward's breath hitched, then he delivered a blow that had Jim staggering back. The collective gasp again struck the air. Then, like his boss, Ward offered a nod and strode after his wife.

"Looks like you failed all around, Taylor." Brown offered a haughty look. "And don't come looking to me for a paycheck."

"I faced down a monster and left with my life." Jim rubbed his stomach. "I think it's time for me to lay low for a while."

No one replied to that, and Jim didn't mind. He eased into the saddle, making sure the Orsons and Wards were on their way out of town before he turned back the way he'd come.

He'd completed his mission. The one from Brown and the one from Ben. Now began a new adventure.

Yes, he planned to keep a low profile, but not in America. He urged his horse into a gallop. He had a train to catch back to Washington, D.C to meet with a certain recruiter, then a ship across the Atlantic, and finally back to Bieldfell. Or Eden Cove. Or the little town near Rotterdam where Ben, Eleanor, and Amalie were making their new home.

He'd go where they needed him. While Ben would continue to go into Germany to rescue children in need, Jim could be the courier taking them from Eden Cove to Bieldfell or whatever safe haven Agnes supplied. Their little corner of the resistance just needed a captain. Someone to ferry those escaping the blackshirts in Italy or brownshirts in Germany across the North Sea to safety.

Jim would do his part, like the others. And pray God would make a way to save as many of His precious little ones as possible. For of such was the kingdom of heaven.

Read on for ...
An excerpt from
The Nanny's Lost Legend
8 Heather Wynd
By Patti Wolf

From the Author

Dear Reader,

Thank you for reading Eleanor and Ben's story. I hope you enjoyed their romance.

If the town of Blue Spruce intrigued you, I invite you to visit Crooked Tooth Ranch and discover the romance between Ben's grandparents in *Heart of Beauty,* a 1870s western retelling of Beauty and the Beast. Find out more at daniellegrandinetti.com/heart-of-beauty.

Then, continue the resistance in *The Italian Musician's Sanctuary*, a stand-alone novella part of Season One: Our House on Sycamore Street. Hunted by one man, can she open her heart to another? Special thanks to Anna Jenson for inviting me to be a part of the original Our House series set in Eden Cove, England. If you'd like to read about the Ferrymans and the beginning of The Resistance forming, you can find out more at daniellegrandinetti.com/the-italian-musicians-sanctuary.

Thank you, too, to Ann Elizabeth Fryer, Sarah Hinkle, and my proofreaders for making this story shine. To Carrie Schmidt for being my first reader as I covered a difficult topic. And last, but certainly not least, a great big thank you to my husband and boys for giving me the time to turn these thoughts into a story for you.

If you've enjoyed *The Recluse's Vindication*, I'd be most grateful if you'd take a moment to leave an honest review. Be sure to join my Fireside News weekly newsletter so you don't miss any details about how the resistance continues: daniellegrandinetti.com/fsn.

Thank you, again, for joining me for Eleanor and Ben's story. To keep in touch, find me at daniellegrandinetti.com.

Happy reading!
Danielle Grandinetti

Excerpt From The Nanny's Lost Legend

CHAPTER ONE ~ *Lizzy*

An autumn breeze whistled through the Highlands of Scotland, tossing the emerald blades of grass about like waves on pristine waters. Surrounding the landscape was lush lavender heather in its late summer growth. My view was breathtaking.

I exhaled. My feet longed to dance a jig that I learned from my homeland, which was not so far from this haven. I closed my eyes to meditate. *Lord, clothe me with Your mercy.* Cobwebs from the past clung to my dark memories, haunted by pain and sorrow. I was free now. Yet somehow nightmares followed me, and memories haunted my days.

My thoughts were vivid as I recalled the journey that brought me to this point.

"Get back, or the ocean will grasp its arms around you to strangle life from you. You did not survive years of famine to faint in the moments of freedom." The burly captain had fiercely chided me days ago. *"Give it a lash, gal. The night will turn to day. If you don't try, you will never know what will come."*

Then, as now, I did not want to know what was next without my family. Just as the ship rocked wildly on my journey to Scotland, so did my raw emotions.

A sound from a string of migrating birds startled me back to reality. The tense recollections vanished as I tumbled to the earth. *I have become one with the Highlands. In and out goes my breath until each sticky strand of web is released from my past. The famine, the fury, and the fear vanished here in the Highlands, not far from the village of Bieldfell, where my ship ported on Loch Ness. Thank you, Lord.*

What new promise or legend would be found tucked away in the folds of Scotland? My heart longed for adventure. It also yearned for the love my parents once had. Their love traveled long like the length of the Scottish lochs that surrounded me now. My faither's deep, rich voice would hum an Irish love song as he and my mam danced hand in hand despite the trials.

Faither would coo in my mam's ear. So many words of love tumbled from his lips.

"My heart's true love.
My eternal beauty, who
will remain in my heart...
until the end of all time.

"I'll sing you a sweet little song...
She is dearer by far,
than the world's brightest star
And I call her my wild Irish Rose."

I knew there were more lyrics, but the ones that counted the most were sung over and over again.

Not many folk tales clung to my Irish lochs. Here in Scotland, it was different. Perhaps that was my sin. For I longed to hear of those legends, and they captured my daily thoughts.

Before me now stretched the wandering waters of Loch Ness. Massive and mysterious in size. It was here that I hoped to see the beloved monster, Nessie. Don't think poorly of me. There was romance in the stories that I'd heard since I was a wee child.

On arriving, I was told of another loch creature; the beautiful Loch Lomond beast. In local taverns, sweet songs are sung of two Scottish brothers who were captured soldiers. They were imprisoned within England's Carlisle Castle near the border of Scotland. Loch Lomond tells the story of how one of them was to be executed while the other was to be set free.

Only the residents know the facts of the great sacrifice and sorrow of the men. The younger brother gave up his life so his older brother could live. As my scars lingered, I could imagine the grief that was left behind. It makes no difference if it's a dearthair *(brother)*, a mam or a faither who is lost on this earth.

Then there's Loch Morar, with its folk tales of Morag. I'm told a beast lurks in the depths of the loch. She's assumed to be beautiful like a mermaid with long-flowing yellow hair. She was a very timid creature. Some say death may come to a member of one's family at the sight of her.

When that happens, Morag wails and weeps over the loss. Her cries are so mournful that local people wake up.

So many legends burned in my heart. As I took in the scent of heather, my soul relaxed. However, an elusive turmoil was buried deep within my soul. I was torn between myth and my Christian upbringing.

I stared at the rugged, earthy landscape. The dramatic mountain ranges and unique lochs created a passionate curiosity within my heart. I am here now, among the Scottish Highlands, where fairy-tale charm lured me into a place of fantasy I'd longed for as I escaped my past. It is here I'd come to stay and would one day die.

Continue Reading in *The Nanny's Lost Legend* by Patti Wolf.

OUR HOUSE on Heather Wynd

BOOK 1: THE LADY'S COMPANION

by Anna Jensen

As companion to the widowed Lady Campbell, Gwenllian Powys journeys to Scotland — where she uncovers secrets to a past she would never have guessed. Will her discovery derail her present? And how will it shape her future?

BOOK 2: THE CONSTANT PRAY-ER

by Caryl McAdoo

The prayers of a righteous man avails much.

Knowing this truth, Kion Avalyn makes praying for his family, friends, and bakery business, the small town of Bieldfell and his ancestral home, No. 2 home on Heather Wynd, his mission in life.

BOOK 3: THE HIGHLANDER'S SECRET

by Rena Groot

Secrets, clan wars, and forbidden love are all wrapped up in The Highlander's Secret. What lies in wait in the shadows of the past, shaped by courage, love, and passion? What will these secrets awaken in the present?

BOOK 4: THE LOVER'S BRIDGE *by Lynn Dean*

In a single weekend, Thom Davidson lost everything--his home, his business, and his fiancee. Embarking alone to the Scottish Highlands, he aims to figure out what comes next and discovers an opportunity beyond anything he ever imagined...but a future in the past demands hard choices.

BOOK 5: THE NESSIE HUNTER'S DIARIES

by Lori Soard

Tessa Carter's great-grandfather told fantastical stories about a monster in the loch. Will his diary reveal more than the ramblings of an old man?
A sweet contemporary romance set against the stunning backdrop of the Scottish Highlands, The Nessie Hunter's Diaries is a story of love, legend, and secrets hidden in the depths.

BOOK 6: THE FREELANCER'S HOPE
by Claire Lagerwall

Abandoned. Forgotten. Alone. At least, that's what Maddie Bennett has always believed. Set against the hauntingly beautiful backdrop of London and rural Scotland, *The Freelancer's Hope* is a powerful story of unraveling lies, rediscovering faith, and learning that even in our deepest pain, God never lets go.

BOOK 7: THE RECLUSE'S VINDICATION
by Danielle Grandinetti

The Loch Ness Monster isn't the only recluse seeking a Scottish haven.

BOOK 8: THE NANNY'S LOST LEGEND
by Patti Wolf

This historical romance is more than bagpipes and loch monsters - love itself may become the greatest monster of all.

BOOK 9: THE WIDOW'S CHOICE *by Francine Beaton*

She's already lost everything once. Can she risk believing in more? In a story of quiet faith, deep loss, and unexpected hope, *The Widow's Choice* explores what it means to stop surviving... and start living.

BOOK 10: THE SISTERS' TOUR   *by Amy Walsh*

Natalie had always believed in happy endings—her parents'
marriage, her father's love, and her own future… until an ancestry
kit shattered everything she thought she knew.

BOOK 11: THE CARER'S CONUNDRUM
by Anna Jensen

She has everything under control. Until she doesn't…
Mary Knight promises to keep her friend, Phoebe's, visit to
London a secret. Until, that is, Phoebe doesn't respond or reply to
Mary's concerned messages and calls. Can Mary keep her secret?
Or will she confide in her favourite patient, Mrs Caldwell —
regardless of the consequences?

BOOK 12: THE BAKER'S PICKLE   *by Vida Li Sik*

Imka's new life in Scotland is blossoming—until her sister arrives,
stirring old tensions and testing faith, family, and forgiveness

BOOK 13: THE TEA MAKER'S BLEND
by Caroline Johnston

He's launching a new tea business; with no time for romance. She's
a gap year student with a pledge not to date. But when a string of
coincidental meetings keep bringing them together, will their
resolve hold?

BOOK 14: THE EXECUTIVE'S DILEMMA
by Allyson Koekhoven

Riley Scheepers — bold, brilliant, and broken — is exiled to the
tiny Scottish village of Bieldfell after one mistake too many. She
was sent away to disappear. Instead, she found herself.

Have you read the first Our House series, Our House on
Sycamore Street?
Travel to Eden Cove and meet the neighbours!
Find the series on Amazon at
amazon.com/dp/B0D7NQHG8H or
amazon.co.uk/dp/B0D7NQHG8H

Join my Fireside News

Grab a spot on my virtual hearth and receive a weekly email filled with bookish content. As a thank you for subscribing, you'll receive a digital copy of my historical romance novelette: *Fire and Water*.

Subscribe Here

Fairytale Retellings

HEART OF BEAUTY

stand-alone origin novella

Discover the origin of Crooked Tooth Ranch in this 1870s western retelling of Beauty and the Beast.

daniellegrandinetti.com/heart-of-beauty

HIS BOSS'S LITTLE SISTER

stand-alone novella in the Apron Strings Tea
Tale multi-author series

A touch of fairy tale, a spoonful of history, and a teacup of hope ... a 1930s historical romance retelling of Hansel and Gretel.

daniellegrandinetti.com/his-bosss-little-siste

r

UNDERCOVER WISH

stand-alone novella, part of the Di Stasio Giornaliste Agency series

A Di Stasio Giornaliste Agency origin story and a retelling of Aladdin and the Magic Lamp.

daniellegrandinetti.com/heart-of-beauty

Our House Novellas

As the world marches toward what will become WWII, visit Our House as we join the resistance.

The Italian Musician's Sanctuary
Romance, history and intrigue at Our House
on Sycamore Street.

Hunted by one man, can she open her heart to another? Eden Cove, England, 1931—Margherita Vicienzo flees Italy pursued by her former fiancé, a member of Mussolini's Blackshirt. Smuggled illegally into England, Margherita is a foreigner at the mercy of strangers. Her limp from an improperly healed broken leg means she has nothing to offer the Ferryman family, who offer her sanctuary, and nothing to appease their son who resents her presence.

Luke Ferryman needs a wife. He wants to marry for love, but carries the weight of his family's generations-old expectations on his shoulders. Though he inherited the role of both baker and ferryman, he knows he can't fulfill both needs once his aging grandparents retire. A wife would help, but not an illegal one like the refugee his matchmaking grandmother is harboring.

As opposite as night and day, Luke and Margherita forge a tentative friendship that grows despite the constant threat of Margherita's discovery. But when strangers appear in the close-knit seaside town, threatening Luke's livelihood and Margherita's safety, the choice between justice and mercy becomes harder. And sacrifice proves the only answer.

The Recluse's Vindication
Rumors, Monsters, and Second Chances at Our House on Heather Wynd

The Loch Ness Monster isn't the only recluse seeking a Scottish haven.

Bieldfell, Scotland, 1933—Falsely accused of murder sixteen years ago, American cowboy Benjamin Ford has chosen to hide out in the Scottish Highlands. Reclusive and not afraid to die, he rescues children out of an increasingly dangerous Germany. When his childhood best friend appears at his door, he's not the boy she remembers.

Eleanor Finch's life ended sixteen years ago. In one horrible day, she lost her dreams, her reputation, and her heart. However, she never gives up the hope of finding her friend, so when she learns of Ben's whereabouts, she leaves all that is familiar to convince him to return home.

But Eleanor isn't the only person searching for Ben. Hunters follow her trail. The thin veil of gossip and rumor may be their only chance of a future ... unless the Loch Ness Monster is real after all.

daniellegrandinetti.com/our-house

Harbored in Crow's Nest

Welcome to Crow's Nest,
where danger and romance meet at the water's edge.
daniellegrandinetti.com/harbored-in-crows-nest

Confessions to a Stranger

Harbored in Crow's Nest, #1
She's lost her future. He's sacrificed his.
Now they have a chance to reclaim it—together.

Refuge for the Archaeologist

Harbored in Crow's Nest, #2
Will uncovering the truth set them free
or destroy what they hold most dear?

Escape with the Prodigal

HARBORED IN CROW'S NEST, #3
*Only a Christmas miracle will save
an unwed mother and the lumberjack protecting her.*

Relying on the Enemy

HARBORED IN CROW'S NEST, #4
*She's protecting her children.
He's redeeming his past.*

Sheltered by the Doctor

HARBORED IN CROW'S NEST, #5
*A fake relationship might keep her safe,
but will it break their hearts?*

Investigation of a Journalist

HARBORED IN CROW'S NEST, #6
*A second chance to set the record straight,
and rekindle a lost love.*

Di Stasio Giornaliste Agency

La Verità con Integrità. Truth with Integrity.
The Legacy of a (Girl) Stunt Reporter.
daniellegrandinetti.com/di-stasio-giornaliste-agency

Undercover Wish

Di Stasio Giornaliste Agency, #0
Alessandra Di Stasio
Chicago World's Fair: World's Columbian Exposition

Eyewitness Sketch

Di Stasio Giornaliste Agency, #1
Gabriella Salatino
Prohibition

Sabotage Games

DI STASIO GIORNALISTE AGENCY, #2

Emma Hancock

Summer & Winter Olympics: Lake Placid & L.A.

Shrouded Trail

DI STASIO GIORNALISTE AGENCY, #3

Lena Carney

Presidential Election

Fraudulent Progress

DI STASIO GIORNALISTE AGENCY, #4

Klara James

Chicago World's Fair: A Century Of Progress Exposition

Pursuing Dust

DI STASIO GIORNALISTE AGENCY, #5

Tabitha Jóhannsson

Dust Bowl

Hostile Ally

DI STASIO GIORNALISTE AGENCY, #6

Liesl Kaufman

Berlin Olympics

Unexpected Protectors

Visit small-town Wisconsin during the Dairy Strikes of the Great Depression in these three historical romances.

For details, visit:

daniellegrandinetti.com/unexpected-protectors

To Stand in the Breach

STRIKE TO THE HEART, #1

She came to America to escape a workhouse prison,
but will the cost of freedom be too high a price to pay?

A Strike to the Heart

Strike to the Heart, #2
She's fiercely independent.
He's determined to protect her.

As Silent as the Night

Strike to the Heart, #3
He can procure anything, except his heart's deepest wish.
She might hold the key, if she's not discovered first.

About the Author

Danielle Grandinetti is an award-winning author of 1930s historical romance, where mystery and suspense intertwine with hope. Her work has received recognition including a Distinguished Faith in Writing Award, two National Excellence in Storytelling Awards, and finalist honors in the FHLCW Reader's Choice, Selah, and Daphne du Maurier contests.

A second-generation Italian-American rooted in Midwest traditions, Danielle draws inspiration from tea, books, and the creative beauty of nature. Holding a master's in communication and culture, and driven by a lifelong love of stories, she crafts tales that celebrate resilience, diversity, and belonging. Danielle lives along Wisconsin's Lake Michigan shoreline with her husband and two sons. Find her online at daniellegrandinetti.com.

www.ingramcontent.com/pod-product-compliance
Lightning Source LLC
Chambersburg PA
CBHW061802190726
48289CB00007B/2037